Fabulous
FATHERS

**He's more than a man—
he's a fabulous father!**

Dear Mattie,

My little girl is growing up. You probably think that I haven't noticed, and it's true that I don't really want to face it, but can you blame me? You're all I've had since your mother died. I can't believe I would even have survived the loss without my darling daughter. But I know that I can't hold you too close. Somehow I have to learn to let you go. Otherwise, I'm sure to lose you. How could I bear that? Already I wonder if I know you sometimes. I ask myself, is that my girl beneath all the makeup and the wild hair? Then I do something foolish, and the young lady who puts me in my place has an uncanny twinkle in her eye, and there's my Mattie, droll and sweet and loving. I miss her sometimes, and yet I know that we have to find our way together to a new kind of relationship, adult to adult. Be patient with me, Mattie. I'm trying. I'm praying for help. The one thing I beg you always to remember is that I love you and always will.

Dad

Fabulous
FATHERS

ARLENE JAMES
Most Wanted Dad

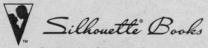

Silhouette® Books

Published by Silhouette Books

America's Publisher of Contemporary Romance

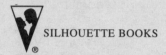

SILHOUETTE BOOKS

Recycling programs for this product may not exist in your area.

ISBN-13: 978-0-373-18887-1

MOST WANTED DAD

Copyright © 1996 by Deborah A. Rather

All rights reserved. Except for use in any review, the reproduction or utilization of this work in whole or in part in any form by any electronic, mechanical or other means, now known or hereafter invented, including xerography, photocopying and recording, or in any information storage or retrieval system, is forbidden without the written permission of the editorial office, Silhouette Books, 233 Broadway, New York, NY 10279 U.S.A.

This is a work of fiction. Names, characters, places and incidents are either the product of the author's imagination or are used fictitiously, and any resemblance to actual persons, living or dead, business establishments, events or locales is entirely coincidental.

This edition published by arrangement with Harlequin Books S.A.

® and TM are trademarks of Harlequin Books S.A., used under license. Trademarks indicated with ® are registered in the United States Patent and Trademark Office, the Canadian Trade Marks Office and in other countries.

Visit Silhouette Books at www.eHarlequin.com

Printed in U.S.A.

ARLENE JAMES

says, "Camp meetings, mission work and church attendance permeate my Oklahoma childhood memories. It was a golden time, which sustains me yet. However, only as a young widowed mother did I truly begin growing in my personal relationship with the Lord. Through adversity He has blessed me in countless ways, one of which is a second marriage so loving and romantic it still feels like courtship!"

The author of more than sixty novels, Arlene James now resides outside Fort Worth, Texas, with her beloved husband. Her need to write is greater than ever, a fact that frankly amazes her, as she's been at it since the eighth grade! She loves to hear from readers, and can be reached at 1301 E. Debbie Lane, Suite 102, Box 117, Mansfield, Texas 76063, or via her Web site at www.arlenejames.com.

Chapter One

It was rude. It was nerve-racking. It was decidedly *un*neighborly. To an inveterate smoker who hadn't had a cigarette in *nine* hours, it was utterly unbearable. No one had answered the door when she had knocked, not that anyone inside that house could have heard anything above the racket booming from what must have been a very impressive set of stereo speakers.

Amy clenched her teeth and pushed her hands through her hair. The new neighbors hadn't been in the house next door a full week yet; she hadn't even laid eyes on any of them, and already she was regretting that they'd ever moved in. She covered her ears with her hands, wondering how anyone could label that shrieking din "music," and considered her alternatives.

She could sit here in her own home huddled in misery, and slowly go insane. She could have a smoke. She could go somewhere else. She could call the police.

No course of action held any appeal, but the last seemed the least objectionable, since it didn't require her to actually get dressed and leave her house at two o'clock in the morning. In truth, the idea would have been no less offensive if it had been two o'clock in the afternoon. Amy liked staying home. She liked her TV programs. She liked her solitude. She liked her cigarettes. But smoking was not an option, however much she wished it was. She had promised her little niece, Danna, that she would quit, and for some reason, a promise to Danna seemed inviolable. Moreover, it was a reason that Amy did not wish to explore or clarify. After all, children had no place in her life. She and Mark had decided that long ago. Mark.

Mark would have known how to handle this situation without resorting to the police. Mark would have strolled over there and charmed the socks off whoever had the audacity to crank up that stereo to such deafening levels. Mark would have had the culprit humming Sinatra and lip-synching Streisand. Mark…who had been her life, who had suffered and died, leaving her so very alone.

It had been over two-and-a-half years since his death, and everyone told her that she was supposed to "be over it" by now, but she missed him still. And yet, something had changed. For a long time she had considered her purpose in life to grieve her husband. Before that she had known that her purpose was to be with him, to make him happy. Now she didn't know what she was supposed to be about. She only knew that the blaring music from next door was about to split her skull, that she was going to go mad if something wasn't done and that it was up to her to do it, because Mark was gone forever. She reached for the telephone. Moments later she was explaining the situation to a dispatcher at the Duncan Police Department.

"That's right, the next to the last house on the end of the street…. No, there's nothing on the other side, just an empty field, and the racket is coming from the last house…. Yes, and please hurry. I'm not feeling well…. No, I don't need an ambulance, just some peace and quiet…. Thank you."

She hung up and leaned forward, elbows on knees, sighing. Her head was pounding. Maybe if she could clear her mind the pain would go away. But when she tried to block all thought, her world became one throbbing ache. She reached instead for the memories that had so often sustained her, memories of the vibrant, charismatic, exciting man who had singled her out for his attention shortly after she'd graduated from high school and had promptly become the center of her universe. For a moment those memories shimmered before her mind's eye as golden and bright as ever. But then they began to darken and change, bringing her instead the sight and sound and smell of the sickroom during the long, downward slide of her husband's health, leaving him broken and dulled, a mere shell of his former self—fragile, thin, pale…querulous, resentful, difficult….

She shook off such thoughts, feeling them disloyal. She wouldn't blame him. She wouldn't. He had been dying, after all, and he had known it. How could he have been anything but resentful? Who could have expected him to remain his old cheerful self when his body had become that of a stranger? And if he had blamed her… Well, he hadn't meant it. She had not put that cancer in his brain, and she had cared for him as tenderly and lovingly as any wife could have. He hadn't known what he was saying. He hadn't even realized that he was hurting her with his accusations and complaints. She wouldn't remember him like that. She wouldn't! Desperately she searched for a distraction, and suddenly the blasting, frenetic music that had only minutes earlier been the bane of her existence became her salvation.

Surging up to her feet, she let righteous anger rise within her. She was going over there to give that cretin a piece of her mind even if she had to beat the door down to do it! Throwing her bathrobe on over the boxer shorts and T-shirt that served as pajamas, she marched toward the door. But just as she wrenched the door open, a police car cruised down the street and braked to a halt in front of the house next door. A tall, powerfully built man in a Duncan City Police uniform stepped out from behind the wheel and strode straight into the offender's house without so much as a knock. Amy was first shocked and then smugly pleased. Obviously she hadn't over-reacted at all. In an instant the music shut off and blessed silence ensued. Feeling vindicated and relieved, she closed the door and sat down to await the officer's report.

Evans stormed into the house, appalled at the din emanat-ing from his very own home. He strode across the narrow entry hall and into the spacious living room, stepping over his daughter on the way to the elaborate stereo system that he had purchased only last Christmas. She rolled over onto her back as he passed, then sat up on the floor as he silenced the noise with a flick of his wrist.

"You're home early."

"I'm not home! I'm on a call, thank you very much! Cripes, a disturbance call at my own house! What are you trying to do, get me fired two days into a new job?"

Mattie bit her lip, her emerald green eyes suddenly wide and childlike beneath the heavy kohl makeup. Evans winced at the sound of his own voice, at the look on her face, at the whole blasted situation. This was supposed to be a new start for them, a way to coax back the little girl that cloaked herself in the rebellious indifference of a modern Chloe. He still cringed when he thought of his little girl with that…that… *musician.*

Evans shuddered, remembering the freak with whom his sweet, generous Mattie had declared herself in love. The only hair on that buffoon's head had been a long, ragged ponytail sprouting from his crown. He'd plucked his eyebrows into a Satanic arch and decked himself with chains that hung from rings piercing his ears and nose, and the only thing he'd worn on his back had been an electric guitar. The very idea of his Matilda being in love with *that* had sent him scurrying for a new position as far from California as possible. He'd lucked into quiet, middle-class, conservative Duncan, Oklahoma, almost immediately, and he'd accepted a demotion in rank, a pay cut, and the worst possible work shift in order to come here. He'd told himself that Mattie would adjust, but so far she'd merely glowered and grumbled and experimented with absurd new shades of color for her lovely, hip-length black hair. Tonight the overtones came in somewhere between purple and burgundy. While he was trying to decide on the exact shade, Mattie's practiced indifference conquered her vulnerability.

"I don't care one way or another about your silly old job," she announced, flopping over onto her belly again and picking up the magazine she had been perusing.

For an instant Evans saw red, but then he tamped down the anger and dredged up as much fatherly concern as he could at the moment. "Maybe you don't care about my job," he said, "but I assume that you still care about *me.*"

She sent a slightly crestfallen look over her shoulder, then shrugged, but her voice was soft with emotion when she said, "You're my father, aren't you?"

He went down on one knee beside her and ruffled her hair as he'd done so often, before she'd started rinsing it with absurd colorations and stiffening it with starch. "Happily, I am," he said, softening his own tone.

She bowed her head. "I didn't think anyone would care. There doesn't seem to be anyone around."

"It's a quiet street," he admitted, "and when you've lived your whole life one on top of another, I guess it takes some getting used to, but we do have neighbors, and they're entitled to sleep nights. Speaking of which, why don't you go on to bed now so that you can get up and have breakfast with me when I come home in the morning?"

She made a noise of disgust. "And spend the rest of my day sitting up alone or tiptoeing around trying not to disturb you? No thanks."

He closed his eyes and began counting slowly to ten. He knew it was a difficult situation, but it wouldn't be forever, and she needed to keep to a conventional schedule. School would be starting soon, and he didn't want her senior year to be more difficult than it had to be. From what he'd seen of the kids around town so far, she was going to have some trouble fitting in as it was. She certainly didn't need to show up every morning dead tired and bleary-eyed. But now was not the moment to raise the issue. He got to ten, took a deep breath and opened his eyes. "Maybe there's something interesting on cable," he suggested. "Or maybe you'd like to start reading that book on local history that I bought—"

"I'll try the cable," she said abruptly, pushing up onto one elbow and reaching for the remote control.

Evans smiled to himself. Score one for reverse psychology. At least he'd gotten the hang of that lately. To think that it had all been so easy once! Mattie had been the light of his life since the day she'd come into this world, and he had once been the center of hers, but he supposed it was natural for her to shift her interests elsewhere. She was seventeen, after all.

Seventeen! Soon she'd be eighteen, and then would come high school graduation and college, he supposed, followed by independence and one day even marriage. As always, when he thought of Mattie leaving him, he felt a vague sense of panic, a flash of the old grief, but it was unfair to think that way and he knew it. She was his daughter, and daughters grew up and left their fathers' homes for lives of their own—eventually. It wasn't a happy thought, though.

His gut clenched every time he thought of Mattie leaving him for good. He'd be utterly alone then. It wasn't as if he didn't want to fall in love again, he just couldn't seem to find the right woman. He shook away the thought and turned his mind back to business. He wasn't just the father or the homeowner here. He was also the officer of record, and as such, he had duties.

He dropped a kiss onto Mattie's discolored head and pushed up to his feet. "I have to go," he said. "I'll check on you in a couple of hours. Try to get some sleep please."

She mumbled something indecisive and fixed her attention on the television screen. Evans walked toward the entry, then paused and turned back.

"By the way, the complaint came from next door."

She rolled onto her side and propped her head on the heel of her hand. "Really? You mean somebody actually lives there?"

"I told you someone did," he reminded her. "She's pretty reclusive, apparently, but she's in there."

Mattie wrinkled her nose. "Probably some old crone who came in during the land rush."

"Whoever she is," Evans remonstrated mildly, "we have to get along with her. She's a neighbor, and you know what the Good Book says about neighbors."

Mattie rolled her eyes. "Yeah, yeah, love thy neighbor, and all that stuff."

"Exactly. Now behave yourself."

She mumbled again, and he had the feeling that he didn't really want to know what she'd said. "See you later, sweetheart."

"See ya."

"And keep the door locked," he called from the entryway.

"Why should I?" she came back. "I thought we were living in the Garden of Eden here."

"There is no Garden of Eden anymore," he told her under his breath, and he locked the door himself when he went out, just to make sure. Then he turned his attention to the house next door and took a deep breath.

Amy switched off the television and got to her feet, thrusting her arms into the sleeves of her bathrobe again as she moved toward the door. She was prepared to be gracious and properly thankful. She was shocked, instead, to find a wildly handsome stranger in the uniform of a city police officer standing on her doorstep. His cap was tucked under his arm, leaving exposed a headful of thick, inky black hair that glistened in the porch light.

He consulted the clipboard in his hands. "Mrs. Slater?"

"Yes."

The clipboard went the way of the cap, then he was extending a hand. "I'm Officer Kincaid, ma'am, Evans Kincaid, and, um, I live next door."

Next door? Amy's mouth fell open. "Oh, my goodness."

He nodded apologetically. "My daughter lives with me. She's seventeen, and you know how seventeen-year-olds are about their music…. Well, anyway, we hadn't seen anyone around this place and she…she thought the place was empty, so…"

Amy had to close her mouth before she could make a reply, and the very idea that she might be gaping at this handsome man for any reason other than outrage was, well, outrageous. "The house is not vacant!" she snapped. "I've lived here four years, I'll have you know."

"Yes, ma'am, and she was making entirely too much noise," he said calmly. "My apologies."

"Well, I should think you would apologize," Amy huffed, feeling inexplicably disturbed, "leaving a child completely unsupervised like that."

"She's not exactly a child," Evans returned. "Her mother was only about six months older than Mattie is now when I married her."

Amy hadn't been much older than eighteen when Mark had swept her off her feet, either, but she heard herself saying snidely, "I expect it's too much to hope your child bride might be able to control her own daughter, then."

Leaf green eyes suddenly blazed, a muscle flexed in his finely sculpted jaw, and even in the dim light on the porch, she could see dull red pulsing beneath his bronzed skin. It occurred to her that she had, indeed, gone too far, but rather than feeling fear or even shame, she felt an odd exhilaration, a kind of *thrill,* as she watched him master his anger. Breathing through his mouth, head slightly bowed, shoulders squared, he very deliberately took control of the emotion so obviously flooding him. In mere moments that sleek, dark head came up and the angry color receded, leaving behind only the flash of fire in yellow-green eyes.

"My wife is dead," he said bluntly, "and my Mattie is as fine a young lady as you'll ever find walking God's green earth! Sometimes playing her music too loud doesn't mean she's out of control! Now, I've apologized, and Mattie will, too, at a more appropriate time. If that's not good enough for you, I suggest you press charges. I'll call another officer to take care of it for you if that's what you want. You just say the word."

Amy blinked at him. She hadn't actually thought of pressing charges. It was just a stereo played too loud. No unauthorized party had been going on, after all. But pride wouldn't quite let her back down, not in front of this proud, handsome man. She lifted her chin. "I'll think about it and let you know."

Those green eyes flashed bright. "You do that. Good night, then, ma'am."

"Good night."

She practically closed the door in his face, then gasped at her own impudence. She couldn't think what had come over her! The poor man probably wanted to strangle her, and him a police officer, no less. A *widowed* police officer. Widowed. They had that in common, at least. She shook her head suddenly. Well, what of it? He might be good-looking, and he might have a quick temper—which he controlled admirably—but what difference did that make if he couldn't even control his own daughter? Without even realizing what she was doing or why, Amy put Evans Kincaid out of mind, choosing instead to concentrate on the daughter. She wasn't thrilled about having a wild teenager living next door without proper adult supervision. The sanctity and peace of her home were all she had left, after all. Was it too much to ask to be able to hear her own television set in her own house? In the middle of the night, no less! Oh, this was not going to work. She could already see that this just would not work, no matter how handsome, er, widowed he was.

Evans forked eggs into his mouth and reached for his coffee cup. Correction, *milk* cup. His daughter had decided that coffee would only keep him awake, and she was probably right about that. He was having enough trouble adjusting to this new schedule as it was, but it took real concentration to keep from making a face as he swallowed the white liquid. Across the table from him, Mattie nibbled on dry toast and sucked her milk through a plastic straw with a ridiculous number of curls and loops in it. He remembered buying her that straw at one of the amusement parks in Southern California. How old had she been then? Nine? Ten? Younger than twelve, for sure, because she had been twelve when her mother had died.

Had it been five years already? Or was it closer to six? Yes, definitely closer to six, for his little girl would be eighteen in October, and this was already the middle of August. He himself had seen forty in June, which meant that Andie would have been thirty-seven in May, though to him she would always be eighteen. She hadn't changed one iota from the sweet, loving girl whom he had married during his senior year in college. Even on the day that drunk driver had jumped the median in his truck and skidded through the crosswalk to knock his Andie all the way through the intersection, she could have passed for a teenager. He wondered what she would have been like now. Certainly not like that crab next door.

Next door.

There was a feud sizzling there, and he had to find a way to defuse it before it exploded in his face. It was the last thing he needed, being new on the job. He sighed mentally, suddenly feeling very tired and every day of forty. He put down both fork and cup and pushed away his plate, looking at his daughter. As usual, she sensed his regard almost immediately.

"What?" she asked, looking up.

"You have an apology to make, young lady, and there's no sense in putting it off."

She was clearly shocked, her mouth dropping open. "You've got to be kidding! It's the crack of dawn!"

He glanced at the clock on the front of the wall oven behind her head. "It's eight thirty-five. The whole world's up." He pushed his chair back. "Come on, let's get it over with."

"Aw, Da-ad!"

"The sooner it's done, the sooner we can get some sleep."

"Rats!" Mattie grumbled, but she got to her feet, slinging her long hair over one shoulder.

Evans frowned at the spiked bangs, but he said nothing. Why comb out the bangs and leave the black eyeliner and the ghost-pale makeup? At least the dark red lipstick had worn off, along with the other makeup that made her look like a vampire. But he knew better than to say so. She'd simply accuse him again of not wanting her to grow up—and she'd be right, darn it.

He opened the back door and marched her through it, then off the porch and across the yard to the fence gate. It was already warm. He could hear a lawn mower farther up the street, but he doubted that would last long. Soon the day would blaze with three-digit heat. He'd been warned about these Oklahoma summers, and everything he'd been told was true. Not having to wear starched khakis in the heat of the day was the only good thing about working the night shift. On the other hand, it would be sundown before he could get to his own lawn, maybe tomorrow. It could go one more day.

The gate swung open easily beneath his touch, and he took pride in its smooth movement. It was one of the first repairs he'd made about the place. He liked to keep things in good shape, himself included. They walked side by side down the narrow drive, his late-model pickup truck safely locked inside the detached garage.

"This is dumb," Mattie said sullenly. "If she was up at two o'clock this morning, she won't be awake yet."

"She will if she'd been in bed for a while before you woke her at 2:00 a.m."

Mattie wrinkled her nose as they turned onto Mrs. Slater's lawn. "But how do you know that?"

"Well, for one thing, she was wearing a bathrobe and, I presume, night clothes when I called on her."

Mattie didn't appear to want to argue with that, settling instead for a shrug. "What if she works? She'll be gone already."

"In that case," he said, stepping up onto the front porch, "you'll have to make this short walk again this evening."

Mattie mumbled something under her breath. He caught and ignored the word *stupid*, not wanting to know whether

it had been applied to him, their new neighbor or Mattie
herself. He rapped smartly on the door, then pushed the
doorbell for good measure. While he was waiting, he
looked around at the front of the house. There was a brick
loose in the border on the empty flower bed at the front of
the porch, and several nails had pulled out of the soffit,
leaving the underside of the eave—which needed
painting—looking dilapidated. He could see a bit of
flashing hanging down at the edge of the roof, too, and one
of the window screens was torn. The place definitely
needed some work.

Mrs. Slater was either single or married to a remarkably
uncaring man.

The door opened, revealing a plump woman with short
brown hair who obviously did nothing to enhance her appearance. Her hair was uncombed, her clothing unkempt, none of
which detracted from her pretty face. In fact, her eyes were quite
stunning, and then he realized he was staring down into them.

"Oh. Ah, I, um, hope we haven't caught you at a bad time."

She pushed a hand through her hair. Her eyelashes were
golden, he noticed, and her eyes a very bright, very clear blue.
She hid a yawn behind her hand. "Don't you sleep, Officer…?"

He tamped down a spurt of irritation. "Kincaid. Evans
Kincaid."

"Ah, yes. Kincaid. And this, I suppose, is your daughter?"
She gave Mattie a swift once-over, her own delicate features
arranged in a frown of obvious disapproval. "You're letting
the air-conditioning out," she said, turning away. "You might
as well come in—now that I'm up."

Mattie shot him a smug look, which he glowered over
before pushing her inside and pulling the door closed behind

him. The odor of stale cigarette smoke immediately assailed him. He cleared his throat, forestalling a cough, and saw that he was standing in the living room. Mattie had her hand over her mouth and nose but dropped it when he signaled her to do so. Mrs. Slater pulled a blanket and a pillow off the couch, making room for them to sit, which they did, side by side. Mrs. Slater pulled the belt of her robe a little tighter and slid over the arm and into the seat of a recliner positioned directly in front of the TV.

"I'd offer you some coffee, but I don't have any made yet," she said, sounding anything but apologetic.

"That's all right," Evans quickly assured her. "We're about to hit the hay ourselves, so coffee's the last thing we need right now."

"Oh, right," she said, "the late shift."

For a long, awkward moment, silence reigned, then Evans nudged Mattie as surreptitiously as possible with his elbow. She swallowed, revealing her nervousness, and sighed. "I'm real sorry about waking you up last night," she said in an endearingly small voice.

Amy Slater flashed a decidedly joyless smile. "Well, to be honest with you, the music *didn't* wake me. The problem was that I couldn't hear my television…and I had a terrific tension headache." She grimaced and blurted, "I'm trying to quit smoking."

Evans felt an absurd sense of relief. "Well, that explains it," he said brightly. She immediately took umbrage, her spine suddenly ramrod straight, her nails digging into the arms of her chair. They were attractively long, he noticed, and painted pale pink. They gave her hands a graceful, feminine look. He wondered if she painted her toenails, too, but before he could look to see if her feet were bare, she was taking him to task with her tongue again.

"If you're implying that the music wasn't too loud, I have to object. My windows were rattling over here!"

"Oh, come now, it wasn't quite that—"

"It was every bit that bad!" she insisted, sliding to the edge of her chair. "It's a wonder that child can still hear!"

Evans strangled a sharp retort, wanting to tell her not to speak of *his* child as *that* child. Instead, he heard Mattie telling her quite calmly that she was *no* child, period.

"And I don't have to stay here and be insulted!" she concluded, getting smoothly to her feet.

Mrs. Slater followed her up. "I didn't insult you! I merely said—"

"Sit down!" Evans barked, surprised when Amy Slater promptly popped back down into her chair. Mattie, at whom his order had been aimed, first folded her arms then gave him a belligerent glare before complying. Evans gulped down further orders and leaned forward, elbows on knees, as he reached for a reasonable tone.

"The music was too loud," he said flatly. "Whether it was as loud as you imply or not, it *was* too loud. We apologize. Let that be the end of it."

"Fine," Amy snipped, lifting her nose and turning her face away.

Evans set his back teeth. "What else would you have us do, Mrs. Slater? There were no physical damages that I can repair, no monetary losses to be incurred. We have apologized. Now, can't we get along as neighbors should?"

Amy waved a hand dismissively. "I'm not the one who tried to blow the neighbor's house off its foundation."

Evans closed his eyes and began to count, then abruptly gave up and took to his feet. "Fine! Let's go, Mattie. We're obviously wasting our time here."

Mattie jumped up and followed him to the door. He went out of it and didn't look back, Mattie at his heels. He'd really wanted to get along. He had *tried* to get along. Well, so much for good intentions! It was just his luck to move in next door to a hardheaded woman in the throes of a nicotine fit. When he heard the slam that indicated Amy Slater had the gall to be angry at him, he clenched his fists and kept walking. He didn't dare comment to Mattie, because if he did, he'd soon be shouting, and that would solve nothing. What he did instead was to fix his mind on the day ahead.

He was going to take a cold shower and crawl into bed for a few hours. That would cool off his temper as well as his body. After a very late "lunch," he'd take a look at that squeaky hinge on the garage door and tinker with the idle on his pickup. Then he'd watch a little TV, stretch and go for a run as soon as the sun set. After that, it would be time to get ready for work. All in all, a relaxing, enjoyable day. He wondered what Mrs. Slater would be doing with her time. Nothing useful, if the condition of her home was any indication. It was none of his business, at any rate. The best he could do from now on was to keep his distance. Stubborn woman! If she'd played her cards right, she could've had her house fixed up in the name of neighborly co-operation, but no, she had to be a shrew. Well, it was no skin off his nose. He had plenty to keep him busy as it was. Her house could fall right down around her for all he cared.

But it was a shame that they couldn't at least be amicable neighbors.

It was a real shame.

Chapter Two

Amy was toweling her hair dry when she heard the first knock. *Who on earth?* she wondered. Her sister and brother-in-law, Joan and Griff Shaw, were out of town for several days so Griff could ride in the rodeo, and they always took Danna with them during the summer. Amy's parents hadn't said anything about coming down from Oklahoma City; they rarely left home anymore. Her best—and if she were honest, only—friend, Ruthie, should have been at work. She was of half a mind to ignore it. After all, who else could it be except some solicitor or… No, he wouldn't, not after the way she'd treated him and his daughter this morning. She sighed, pondering again her reaction to her new neighbor. What was it about him that made her want to jump up and run in the opposite direction? It had to be simply a matter of bad timing. He'd come along just when she was trying to quit smoking. Yes, that was undoubtedly it.

Her caller proved persistent, so much so that she finally stuck her head out of the bathroom door and shouted, "Just a minute!" Grumbling, she pulled on denim shorts and a worn, white T-shirt, tugged a comb through her hair, and went barefoot to the door. She couldn't believe it when she opened up and found that it was, indeed, *him* standing there. He wore running shorts, a skimpy sleeveless "muscle" shirt and athletic shoes without socks. The man was obviously in fine physical shape. His lower arms and legs, she noticed, were dusted with fine black hairs, and so, too, she suspected, was his upper chest. For some reason that seemed strangely…erotic. Mark, she recalled, had been inordinately proud of his full head of sandy brown hair, but he'd hardly sported a hair on any other part of his body. Now why would she compare the two of them?

"I was hoping that we could start over," Evans Kincaid was saying.

Amy shook her head to clear it, a movement that Kincaid interpreted as a refusal of his truce. He rolled his eyes, threw up his hands and started to turn away. Impulsively Amy reached out to stop him. This morning's fiasco could be laid squarely at her feet, after all. "Don't go," she said, her hand clamped down over his forearm.

Surprised, he looked at her hand, then lifted his head to beam upon her a smile so bright that it was blinding. "Well, all right."

She snatched her hand away, suddenly feeling ridiculously shy and disheveled. Her hand crept up to her drying hair. "Um, maybe you'd better come in."

He stepped inside and closed the door. "Now what?" she wondered, unaware that she'd spoken aloud until he chuckled.

"Ah, how about a cool glass of water?"

"Oh. Right." Now she was laughing. "Come on back to the kitchen." She signaled for him to follow and turned away to pad across the living room, past the dining suite, and into the hall. She pulled the door to her bedroom closed, not wishing him to witness its clutter, then turned left into the kitchen. "Actually, I have some iced tea if you'd prefer that."

"Tea would be great."

She opened a cabinet door, realized there were no clean glasses there and went to the dishwasher, hoping she'd remembered to run it. Thankfully she had, though she couldn't remember exactly when that might have been. Taking the tea pitcher from the refrigerator, she dropped a few ice cubes into the glass and poured it full. "It's already sweetened. Would you like some lemon?"

He shook his head, then sipped the tea and promptly nodded. "Guess I'd better have lemon, after all."

"Too sweet?" Her mother had always told her that she made syrup, not tea.

He nodded apologetically. "A little." Obviously it was a lot too sweet.

She rummaged in the refrigerator for a lemon, eventually finding a few dried up slices in a tiny bowl. Biting her lip, she closed the refrigerator and suggested that he might prefer water, after all.

"Oh, this is fine," he said unconvincingly, whereupon she snatched the glass out of his hand and dumped its contents into the sink. Quickly she rinsed the glass, filled it partway with water and carried it to the freezer for a couple of ice cubes.

"Thank you," he said when she handed him the glass of water. "May I take a seat?"

"Of course."

He pulled out a chair at her dinky kitchen table and sat down. "Won't you join me?"

She pulled out another chair and sat.

He ran a fingertip around the lip of his glass. "I, um, thought perhaps that if we got to know each other a little better we could, ah, get along."

Amy passed a hand over her eyes. "I get along just fine with all my other neighbors."

"Are any of them teenagers with only one parent and that one of the opposite sex?"

Amy grimaced. "No. Actually there isn't another soul on this whole block under fifty."

He grinned. "I know. It was the deciding factor in the purchase of my house."

She gave him an openly curious look. "Want to explain that?"

He nodded. "Actually, I do." He sipped from his glass and set it down again. "I hoped this neighborhood would have a…calming effect on my daughter. You see, Mattie was just twelve when her mother died."

"Tough age," Amy muttered.

"Very. She was an early bloomer, deep in the throes of puberty. We were very close, Mattie and I, from the day of her birth. I couldn't wait to have a child. Neither could Andie. In fact, we were married in October and Mattie was born just a year later."

"I take it there were no others," Amy commented lightly.

He sighed. "Nope. We always intended to have another, but Mattie was just everything we could have possibly asked for, and we didn't want her to share her early childhood with a sibling. We always had it in the back of our minds to have

another when she started school, but then Andie started
thinking about going to college—I think I told you that she
was only eighteen when we married. Anyway, I thought she
ought to have the chance to go, so when Mattie started school,
so did Andie, and, well, she loved it, so much so that after she
finally got her bachelor's degree, she started in on her
master's. She always said we'd have that second baby before
she hit forty. But she hardly got past thirty." He stared at his
glass, watching the condensation bead on the outside. "She
was crossing the street to her car after class and some hopped-
up frat pledge jumped the median and mowed her down."

"I'm so sorry," Amy said gently.

He nodded, keeping his gaze on his glass. "I couldn't
believe it. It was the worst thing that ever happened to me,
but Mattie… She and her mother were practically insepara-
ble just then. She was suddenly becoming a young lady, and
Andie was so good with her. To tell you the truth, I was
feeling kind of left out. They were always giggling together
and trying on makeup and God knows what all. And suddenly
Andie's gone." He shook his head and sat up straighter in his
chair, finally lifting his gaze. "Mattie's a good girl, Mrs.
Slater, but she's been through a lot. Losing her mother sort
of knocked her off kilter, and she doesn't seem to have ever
really gotten back in balance. She's going through this stage
right now, rebellion, I guess, and there was this boy back in
California…" He told Amy about the rocker, which explained
Mattie's rather bizarre style of fashion. "Actually, the whole
scene was pretty rough out there, gangs and all. When I con-
ceived this notion of moving her out of that climate, I went
to my pastor," Evans said, "and he agreed that it might be best.
Turns out that he's from Oklahoma, and he has a brother on

the force here in Duncan, and the brother had mentioned that one of the captains here was leaving. Well, it seemed heaven-sent. So here we are."

"I take it the move was rather sudden," Amy surmised.

"Yeah, too sudden maybe."

"School will start soon," she told him. "Mattie will make friends."

"I know, I know. And I'll eventually get off this horrible shift, so we can have a real home life again. The new man always starts at the bottom of the totem pole, you know. The original captain on this shift got promoted when the guy I actually replaced left."

"So you got the ugly shift."

"Right. But it's not too bad, really. Things are real calm in Duncan compared to the suburbs of L.A."

"I can just imagine."

He grinned. "Yeah? Have you ever lived in a big city?"

"Actually, I have. I grew up in Oklahoma City, and Mark and I lived in Houston for a while."

"Mark?" He made the question in his voice sound utterly innocent, but those leaf green eyes were anything but. She got a taste of what a criminal suspect must get when being inter-rogated by Officer Kincaid. Oddly, she didn't find the expe-rience unpalatable.

"My husband," she said, then heard herself adding, "my *late* husband."

"Oh," he said, shifting forward in his seat. "Then you're widowed, too."

"Yes," she admitted, her tone closing the door on further inquiry. One dark brow quirked upward at that, but he was a man who could take a hint, apparently, for he said not another word, which was good. Or so Amy told herself. Her relationship with Mark was much too precious to be trotted out for examination with everyone who walked through her door. So why did she feel this niggling sense of disappointment?

Maybe she just needed to talk about Mark, but if so, she'd do her talking to Ruthie. Ruthie had appreciated Mark; she'd been half in love with him herself by the time he became ill. If no one else close to her seemed to have understood him, well, that was their loss. At any rate, she didn't intend to discuss the matter with another man, not this one, anyway. That being the case, she decided to get the conversation back on the proper track. "What happened this morning was my fault," she said flatly. "It's the smoking—or rather, the *not* smoking."

"I'm sure it's very difficult," he said consolingly.

"It certainly is."

"But it's a good thing," he added quickly. "Giving up cigarettes is a very positive move."

"I hope so," she muttered doubtfully.

"What made you decide to quit?"

She grimaced. "I don't know. Well, actually, yes, I do. I have a little niece named Danna, and her parents put her up to bugging me about it. At least, I think they did. They're big health nuts these days, which is pure irony considering who her father, uh, stepfather is. His name's Griff Shaw, the bull rider. Maybe you've heard of him?"

"Griff Shaw! No kidding? Heck, yeah, I've heard of him. Fancy that, Griff Shaw's your brother-in-law. I'll have to remember to tell Mattie that. But, uh, what's this irony business about?"

"Well, before Griff married my little sister, Joan, he was a first-class lush."

"Really? He's an alcoholic then?"

Amy wrinkled her nose. "No, nothing like that. He was just wild, you know, partying all the time."

"Ah, the celebrity life-style."

"Something like that."

Evans Kincaid cocked his head to one side. "It's always struck me odd how these pro athletes sabotage themselves sometimes. I mean, you'd think they'd do everything in their power to protect their primary assets, which logically would be their bodies."

"I suppose," Amy said pensively. "I never really thought about it."

"Hmm, on the other hand, though," Evans went on, "our bodies are of prime importance to all of us, not just the pros. That's why I never could understand why people would subject themselves to the abuse of drugs and such. I mean, if you want a good high, why not exercise? It feels great, and it's healthy." He shook a finger at her, his eyes alight with the glow of inspiration. "Come to think of it, a regular exercise plan might be just what you need to help you get over the craving to smoke, and it'll help with the weight gain, too."

Amy's mouth fell open. He'd as much as told her she was fat, as if she didn't already know. "You rat! What makes you think I care what you think of me?"

He blinked at her. "I beg your pardon?"

"Are you this insensitive with your suspects? I suppose a little exercise would take away the urge to steal or lie or cheat or…or…whatever!"

He was gaping. "I don't know what you're talking about!"

"I'm talking about that cheap crack about my weight!"

"What crack? All I meant was that a lot of people worry about putting on weight when they quit smoking."

"I heard what you said! Oh, just get out of my house!" She jumped to her feet and slammed her chair up under the table.

Evans was still gaping, but he got up and gave his chair the same treatment she had given hers. "Of all the touchy, loony dames! Lady, you take the proverbial cake!"

Amy pointed toward the living room, arm rigid, face livid. "I suggest you take your leave through the proverbial door, *boor,* and don't bother coming back with one of your lame apologies!"

"Oh, don't worry!" he told her, wild-eyed. "I won't be apologizing this time! Any apologies due this time are yours!"

"Ha! I've done all the apologizing I intend to do, period. Now get out!"

"My pleasure," he said, sneering, "and from now on, if you want to talk to me, call the police!"

"Out!" she screamed, but she was talking to an empty space, a fact to which a slamming door attested.

He wasn't gone three seconds when she covered her face with her hands and began to cry. The moment she realized what she was doing, she sniffed up the tears and determinedly bottled them inside of her. She wouldn't cry over a snide remark by a cad like Evans Kincaid. Heavens, she couldn't even remember the last time a man had made her cry.

"For Pete's sake, Amy, what are you trying to do, kill me? Do you want me to die?"

"You know I don't!"

"Then be a little more careful. I'm only your husband, after all."

She shook away the memory. That didn't count. Mark

hadn't known what he was saying. It was the illness talking, the pain. Evans Kincaid was just being hateful when he'd said she was fat. Mark would never have said anything so personal.

"You aren't going out like that, *are you? What if someone I know sees you?"*

Well, of course, Mark commented from time to time. It was his right as a husband, after all, and any comments Mark had made about her appearance he had made for her own good, out of love. Evans Kincaid was just being mean when he'd said what he'd said, no matter how innocent it might have sounded to a third party. Anyway, even if he hadn't actually said that she was fat, he'd certainly *implied* it. Just because he was built like the Rock of Gibraltar he thought he could make snide remarks about everyone else. So what if she'd put on a few pounds? It was her business. She folded her arms and huffed, trying to hold on to her outrage, but reason was slowly returning, and with it came the knowledge that she had again made a fool of herself. She closed her eyes, seeing herself as Evans must see her, a plain, pudgy, high-strung, pathetic excuse for a woman.

She wanted to run next door and beg his pardon, but she wasn't about to give him the satisfaction. What difference did it make, anyway? He was never going to give her another chance, and why should she care? He wasn't anything to her, nothing at all, and that's the way it should be. But for some reason she wanted to crawl back into bed and pull the covers over her head. Why not? What else did she have to do?

It was going on midnight when she realized that the music she was hearing was not part of the television program she was watching. A quick muting of the volume on the set told her unequivocally that the sound was coming from the Kincaids'. It wasn't as loud as before, but it was definitely *too* loud. Amy chewed her lip, wondering what her best course of action might be. Should she let it go and hope it didn't happen again, or ought she try to nip this thing in the bud before it went any further? She hated to go through another scene with Evans Kincaid, but maybe if she moderated her replies this time, if she didn't let him get to her, they could have a reasonable conversation—and maybe she could even find the words to apologize *again*.

She went to the phone, but this time she looked up the non-emergency number and left a personal message for Captain Kincaid, saying that his next-door neighbor was calling to suggest that he swing by his house to take care of a certain situation there. She hardly had time to go over in her mind what she would say to him, when he pulled up in the police cruiser. He slammed his door with his usual gusto and stalked into the house. The music shut off, and a few moments later she heard him and Mattie shouting at one another. After some minutes another door slammed, and Amy thought for certain that he would be on her porch at any moment, but he didn't come.

Amy went to the dining room window and stared out at the house next door. The police cruiser was still parked in the drive, but the house was now dark and silent. A movement of shadow against the yellow light of the Kincaids' front porch told her that Evans was there, perhaps on his way to the car. A moment of indecision passed before she hurried into the living room, thrust her feet into a pair of thong sandals that she kept by the door and went out. The thong broke on one shoe as she was going down the steps. Thoroughly disgusted, she kicked off both sandals and hurried across the dark yard. She had turned down the Kincaids' drive toward the street when she heard what sounded like a man groaning. Stopping in her tracks, she held her breath listening.

"Oh, God," he was saying, "what's happening to us? I prayed and prayed before making this move, and I really thought it was the right thing to do, but now I don't know. I can't even talk to my own daughter anymore. Our next-door neighbor hates us. The shift I'm working doesn't seem to leave time for much of anything else. I don't know what to do now. You have to help me, Lord. I don't seem able to do this on my own. How I wish Andie were here—or someone…."

Amy quietly turned and walked back to her own house, feeling small and ashamed and utterly selfish to be so disturbed by something as common as music played a little too loud, when people like Evans Kincaid had real problems, problems so deep that he prayed about them on his front porch in the middle of the night.

Our next-door neighbor hates us.

She bowed her head as she recalled those words. Her sharp tongue and personal sensitivity had given him that notion. Indeed, what else could he think when she jumped all over him for every innocent remark he made in her presence. She was too ashamed to apologize, but she made up her mind to be a good deal more pleasant in the future—provided he ever spoke to her again. She couldn't blame him if he didn't. In fact, she'd be amazed if he did.

It was ninety-five degrees in the shade, and she wanted to get home in time for the early-evening news, so of course her six-year-old domestic sedan overheated while she was waiting at the red light at the intersection of 81 and Main. Making matters worse, she had just come from the grocery store and could already hear her cottage cheese spoiling, her lettuce wilting and her new low-cal frozen dinners melting. So much for the new diet. Naturally, she was in the inside lane, intending to turn left onto Main Street when a high, whining noise first alerted her to the problem, and that was exactly where the car engine died. She knew the moment she lifted the hood that the problem was well beyond her scope of experience and knowledge. In fact, all she could do was slam the hood down again to keep boiling water from spewing in every direction.

She was standing in front of the car, watching the water from her radiator roll down the street, while other cars whizzed by and an attendant from a nearby service station watched from the doorway of his business. She supposed she'd have to walk over there and ask his advice, though how she could get her car into his service bay was beyond her. It would have to be pushed backward, going in the wrong direction on that side of the street. And pushing that heavy, full-size sedan was certainly more than she could ever manage alone. She didn't see any other alternative, however—until a red, late-model, one-ton pickup pulled up in the lane behind her, and the tinted window on the driver's side silently lowered.

"Blow your radiator cap?"

Amy looked at Evans Kincaid's handsome face and felt her heart drop. "Hi. Um, I don't know. It seems to be coming from behind the radiator."

He nodded and drew back inside. For a moment she thought he would leave, now that he knew who the motorist in distress was, but then the hazard lights on the pickup truck began to blink, the door opened, and Kincaid stepped out onto the curb. He was wearing a red-and-white ball cap and black sunshades, faded blue jeans without a belt and a plain white T-shirt with the tail tucked in. On his feet were black, round-toed cowboy boots. He carried an open cola can in one hand and a rolled up length of leather in the other. As he drew near, Amy could see that he needed a shave. He was the best-looking and the most welcome thing she'd ever seen. He hadn't even done anything, and she felt inordinately grateful.

"Let's take a look," he said. "It ought to be blown out by now, judging by the size of that puddle."

He seemed to know exactly what he was doing, for he handed her the can, walked to the driver's door, opened it, ducked inside and pushed the hood release. He took the can back as he strolled around to the front of the car and lifted the hood. Amy could hear a high-pitched whine and see a tiny fountain of water spewing up.

"Hose," he said succinctly. "It'll have to be replaced."

Amy wrung her hands at that news. "How am I going to do that?"

"No problem," he said. He tilted his head back and took a long drink of the cola, then crushed the empty can in his hand. "Wait here," he said, thrusting the rolled piece of leather at her, "and hold this."

It was inordinately heavy, and she realized as he strolled back toward his truck that some sort of tools were rolled up inside. She held the bundle in both hands and stood there perspiring on the side of the road while he disappeared through the opened door of his truck. After several minutes, he emerged again and walked back toward her.

"Okay," he said, "it's coming."

"What's coming?" She looked up into the opaque black lenses of his glasses.

"The hose and enough antifreeze to replace what's on the ground."

For a long moment she could only stare. "How on earth did you manage that?"

He shrugged. "I used my car phone to call a fellow I know at one of the parts houses in town. Hope you can pay for it when it gets here."

She bit her lip. "Suppose he'll take a check?"

Evans Kincaid grinned. "Oh, I think we can persuade him. It's not like he couldn't find you if it bounced."

"I guess not," she muttered, "living next door to a cop."

He tilted his head. "Has its advantages." She opened her mouth to say she was aware of that fact, but he turned and walked away, saying, "Next order of business is to clear this street."

While she watched, he went to the light pole at the side of the intersection, inserted something from his pocket into a metal box mounted on the side and moved something. The light began to blink red in all directions, bringing traffic to a complete halt. Everything happened quickly after that. Suddenly there were three young men pushing her car through the intersection and onto the parking lot of a car wash. Evans pulled his truck up beside it. The traffic light was reset, and the normal flow of traffic resumed. The man from the parts store came and took Amy's check without the slightest hesitation, saying that from the looks of the puddle in the street, she had diluted her antifreeze too much. She nodded, wondering how she had managed that, then watched as Evans flushed out the radiator with a water hose borrowed from the car wash before exchanging the new radiator hose for the busted one. When that was done, he poured half a container of antifreeze fluid into the radiator, filled the container with water and emptied the whole of it into the system.

"Now then," he said, fixing the cap in place and lowering the hood. "Next time it needs more fluid, you mix two parts antifreeze and one part water and put that in. You don't just add plain water. Understand?"

"I think so."

"Has it been getting hot fairly often?"

"Occasionally."

"And when it did, you put plain water in it," he stated matter-of-factly. "That's how it got too diluted."

"I'm sure you're right," she told him meekly.

"If it happens again, you may want to look into having your thermostat replaced," he advised. Wiping his small wrenches clean with a handkerchief from his back pocket, he slid them back into the proper pockets, rolled up the leather case and tied it closed. "That ought to do for now."

Without another word he walked over to his truck and got in. Amy hurried after, catching the door before he could close it.

"Evans!"

He slid his shades off and dropped them into a console between the bucket seats. "Yeah?"

"I'm sorry," she said. "I mean, I'm sorry for…well, for everything, and thank you for helping me out today. I don't know what I'd have done if you had passed me by—and you had every right to."

He dropped his gaze. "Well, I just always figured that neighbors were supposed help out one another."

"You're right, of course," she told him softly. "I've behaved terribly. I hope this means that you've forgiven me."

He flashed her a grin. "I always forgive pretty ladies." He settled himself behind the wheel then, while her mouth hung open, he said, "I've got to run. Got to shave off this sandpaper before I report to the station." He rubbed his jaw.

She backed up, and he closed the door. Only as the truck was moving did she think to call out, "Thank you!" She doubted that he heard her. The truck had already wheeled out into the street and was accelerating through a green light. In another moment it disappeared over a slight rise in the street.

She stood in the parking lot, her groceries ruining in the back of her car, and wondered if he'd realized what he'd said. He didn't *really* think she was pretty…did he?

Chapter Three

Amy stared at the open pack of cigarettes on the coffee table and imagined herself slipping the filter tip between her lips. She could almost smell the oily fragrance of the flame as she struck the lighter. She could almost feel the swirl of smoke expanding in her lungs, the shiver of nicotine euphoria that seemed alternately to tighten then relax her skin. She closed her eyes and pulled again, shocked to feel pressure on the tip of her little finger rather than the soothing inhalation of smoke. With a groan of disgust, she jerked her hand from her mouth and thrust it through her hair as the hard twang of a rock guitar throbbed through the night. Was it her imagination again, or had the volume been cranked up another notch?

Sighing, she leaned forward on the couch, laid her forehead against her knees and folded her arms over the back of her head. Why was she doing this? Why in blue blazes didn't she just pick up the phone and get Kincaid to come home and take care of this insanity? But she already knew the answer to that. She didn't want to fight with him anymore. She owed him for fixing her car that afternoon…and he had implied that he thought she was pretty, darn him. But that was just casual talk, the sort of thing an attractive, confident man tossed about whenever a woman was around.

Still, she couldn't help wondering how long it had been since any man had commented favorably on her looks. Even Mark hadn't been given to easy compliments. That being so, she would treasure them all the more, he had told her, and of course, Mark was right, which meant that she was being an idiot about this. No meaningless compliment was worth enduring the nerve-jangling blasts from the house next door. She *had* to do something before she started climbing the walls. It was bad enough to want a smoke at this time of night. No one should have to endure this screeching nonsense on top of that.

She got up off the couch, full of righteous indignation, and marched toward the door. On the way she did something she never did, she glanced in the gold-framed mirror on the living room wall, the one Mark's aunt had given them. She shuddered at what she saw. Her hair had grown limp with perspiration. Her cheeks were reddened from being out in the sun, and she had no eyebrows or eyelashes at all. Had she been walking around like this all the time? Maybe she didn't have anybody to impress, but it didn't hurt to take pride in one's appearance. In fact, someone had recently told her that it was healthy to do so. Her sister maybe? It didn't matter. All that mattered was that she not go out this way, no, not even to put that little freak next door in her place.

She made an about-face and marched straight into the

bathroom. By the time she rinsed and dried her hair, slapped on a little foundation, brushed color on her lashes and brows—which turned out to need a little plucking—and stroked on some lip gloss, the music from next door was threatening to break the glass in the windows. What on earth did that child think she was doing? She was practically begging for trouble. Well, trouble was on its way.

Head high, Amy stomped out of the house. This time when she glanced in the mirror, she gave herself a congratulatory nod. Maybe she wasn't drop-dead gorgeous, but at least she was relatively well groomed. She walked across the lawn and Kincaid's drive, then onto the grass in his yard and up onto the porch. She couldn't help noticing that the lawn was clipped and edged. Moreover, the grayish-blue-and-white house was freshly painted and in good repair. The welcome mat was clean, and the porch light was free of insect remains and cobwebs. Somebody had been busy. It was a wonder, though, that the windows weren't in shards and the roof bouncing a foot or so above the walls. How did that kid stand it?

Without bothering to knock, Amy tried the doorknob. It turned freely, and she pushed it open, shouting, "Mattie? Mattie!"

Her hands over her ears, she hurried through the graceful entry and into the living room. Her feet sank into lush softness as she stepped onto the pale gray carpet. A quick scan of the room showed her two things, an impressive stereo system arranged on shelving mounted on one wall and Mattie curled up in a ball in big, comfy club chair, her arms wrapped around her head. Amy launched across the room and started hitting buttons and dials until blessed silence descended. The relief was almost physical.

"Oh, you're home," Mattie said sullenly and lifted her head, which showed definite highlights of green around the face this night. The shock on that face when she saw Amy rather than her father, coupled with the black and green makeup on her eyes and the coral lipstick on her mouth, was downright comical. "What are you doing here?" she asked Amy.

"Saving your hearing. What in heaven's name did you think you were doing?"

Mattie stuck her chin out at a belligerent angle. "You can't just walk in here," she insisted.

Amy chuckled. "Like you'd have heard me if I'd knocked, especially since I screamed for you before I came in."

Mattie glared. "Where's my father?"

"I wouldn't know. Why do you ask?"

Mattie's eyes grew round and shimmering. *She's lonely,* Amy found herself thinking.

"Didn't you call him?" she asked Amy.

"No, I didn't call him. I figure he has enough to do at the moment, keeping the city safe from delinquents like you."

Suddenly Mattie's eyes were flowing with tears. She ducked her head on a strangled sob. Amy melted like butter in summer sunlight. "Hey, now, I was only kidding."

"I'm not a delinquent! I'm not!" Mattie sobbed.

The poor kid's misery pulled Amy across the room. Soon she was standing beside the big jewel-toned chair. "I said I was only kidding. Listen, I won't say a word to your father, I promise."

"Oh, swell!" Mattie snapped, lifting her head and swiping at tears. "Just let him ignore me, see if I care!"

Amy's freshly drawn brows rose straight up. "Is that what

this is all about? You wanted me to call him, didn't you? You wanted him to come home."

Mattie instantly sobered and matured. "Don't be silly. I was just enjoying my music. I don't know why everybody makes such a big deal about it."

Amy folded her arms, smirking. "Right. You always enjoy your music with your ears covered."

The child was back, eyes wide, chin wobbling. "I—I just fell asleep, that's all."

"Yeah? Well, that's some trick. Maybe you could market your secret to a grateful world of insomniacs."

That wobbling chin jutted up stubbornly. "Why are you being so mean to me?"

Amy dropped her jaw in comic outrage. "Me, be mean to you? Have I tried to burst your ear drums? Have I filed public nuisance charges? Have I purposefully blasted you out of your own house?" The operative word, and they both knew it, was *purposefully.*

Mattie dropped her chin to her chest. For some time she said nothing, and Amy sensed that this was a moment when she ought to keep her own mouth shut. Even when Mattie began to quietly cry, Amy kept her silence, and finally Mattie came out with it.

"I don't know what the matter is with me. I don't really want to go back to L.A. To tell you the truth, it really wasn't much better. I just get so lonely sometimes."

Amy felt an instant, unexpected kinship with this odd girl. If anyone understood loneliness, Amy did. She resisted the uncommon urge to lay a hand on Mattie's head and said, "I suppose that's to be expected, but you'll get used to it."

"Get used to being lonely?" Mattie said with some surprise.

Amy was taken aback. Had she really said that? Was that what she'd done, resigned herself to loneliness? She shook her head, as much in answer to her own thoughts as Mattie's. "What I meant to say was that you'll get used to living in a new place a-and that in a couple weeks you'll make some new friends and—"

Mattie threw up her hands and uncurled, sending both feet to the floor. "You're talking about school, but school is so lame! I wouldn't even go if I didn't *have* to."

"Well, you do have to," Amy said, sounding for all the world like her own mother, "so why don't you make the best of it? You might be surprised."

"Don't you understand?" Mattie said desperately. "I need more than school chums!"

"That's right," Amy said. "You need an education." Mattie snorted inelegantly at that, and Amy found herself feeding her the same line adults always fed teenagers. "You can't do anything without an education." Mattie pressed her mouth into a thin line as if refusing a dose of bitter medicine. Amy rolled her eyes in exasperation. "Don't you have any plans, any dreams? What do you want to do with your life?"

Mattie shrugged. "I don't know. I just know that I'm not going to find what I need in some high school."

"Just give it a chance," Amy urged.

"I need something more than most kids my age," Mattie went on. "I need…"

"A mother?" Amy asked softly. Boy, did she know how it felt to need someone who just wasn't there and never would be.

Mattie got a faraway look in her eye, a look tinged with sadness and laden with memories, a look that spoke volumes about her feelings for and need of her mother, but then she shook her head. "It's even more than that," she said huskily. "See, Mom's always with me." She tapped her chest. "She's in here, and nothing can ever take her away. In fact, you could say that she's more 'with me' than Dad is most of the time."

Aha, thought Amy, *we come to the crux of the problem.* And she knew just what to do about it, but it wouldn't do to be too obvious. She put her hands on her hips and looked around her, noting the neatness and cleanliness of the room. Not only did it look clean, it felt clean, even smelled clean, and yet it had a comfortable, homey feel about it. Maybe she ought to move halfway across the country, she thought wryly, but something told her that there was more to it than that. "On second thought," she said, keeping her face as expressionless as possible, "I really don't think I can just let this go by. Maybe you'd better show me where the phone is."

Mattie's expression was one of confusion. Amy could see that having her father brought home was what Mattie wanted, but the fact that the homecoming was apt to bring acrimony now mattered to her when it hadn't before. Then the confusion cleared, and Amy saw real regret…and pride. Mattie wasn't about to beg her not to call. Instead, she lifted a hand and pointed across the room to the formal dining area. "Through there to the kitchen. It's on the right side of the door."

Amy nodded her thanks and went off on her own into the other part of the house. The kitchen was larger and brighter than hers and spotless. A bowl of fruit sat in the middle of the table, and decorative tea towels were draped over the handles of the double wall oven. The place smelled of cinnamon and coffee, just as her mother's kitchen had always done. You didn't get *that* by moving.

She turned to the telephone and lifted the receiver. Several numbers were listed on the interior pad beneath. Beside each was a single boxed digit. Evans's work number was the first. Amy pushed the star button and the number one. When the other party answered, she explained merely that she was Evans's next-door neighbor and that she needed to speak to him. When the man on the other end of the line asked if she wanted to be "patched through," she said that she did. Seconds later she was talking to Evans Kincaid himself.

"There's nothing to be upset about," she told him smoothly, "but I'm at your house with Mattie. Do you suppose you could drop by, on your break maybe?"

"Is she okay?" he asked immediately.

"Physically, she's just fine," Amy assured him, "but could we discuss this in person please?"

"Hold on."

He returned several minutes later to say that he'd arranged to take an early break and would be there in five minutes. Satisfied, Amy went back to the living room, where she encountered a glum Mattie. "Is he coming?" she asked.

"In five minutes," Amy announced. "I'd like a private word with him, if you don't mind."

Mattie's expression became downright hostile, but she acquiesced coldly, saying, "Fine! I'll be in my room. Just make yourself at home. You do, anyway."

Amy contained a smile as Mattie flounced away. Then she did just what Mattie had suggested, curling up in the very chair Mattie had vacated. It was really a very lovely place, and someone had obviously tended it lovingly. Evans? she wondered. Or Mattie? Evans seemed the capable sort, but Amy sensed that Mattie was responsible for the order and comfort of the home. Her eyes narrowed with the germ of an idea. Almost before she knew what was happening, Evans opened the door and walked in.

"Where is she?" he demanded.

Amy looked toward the little hallway that flanked the dining room, then stood. "Maybe we'd better step outside for a moment. We need to talk before you see her."

Evans put his hands on his hips and struck a cryptic pose as if about to refuse, but then he swung out an arm in invitation and acceptance. "After you."

Amy walked out onto the porch, Evans behind her. It was a soft night, she realized, a warm, soft night, a night with purpose. She was struck suddenly by the realization that it had been a very long time since she'd had any purpose at all.

Evans came to stand beside her at the porch rail. "Ready to tell me what this is all about?"

She was more than ready. She was eager. She turned to face him, leaning a hip against the rail. "Mattie was playing the music too loud again. I mean, *way* too loud."

He was instantly angry. "For pity's sake! What's wrong with her? She knows I can't afford to have these kinds of complaints called in!"

"No complaint was called in," Amy said quickly, "not by me, anyway."

His surprise actually shamed her. She had to drop her eyes. "This time I came over and spoke with her, and… You may think I'm sticking my nose in where it doesn't belong, but I thought you should know… She misses you."

He was silent for a moment, and then he said, "What do you mean, she misses me. I'm right here."

"Are you?" Amy asked softly, daring to look up again. "I mean, you must be pretty busy, a single father with a new job in a new place. Do you really have the time for her that you used to?"

He began a glare, but it turned thoughtful before it developed much intensity. "You know it wasn't so long ago," he said in a near whisper, "when she didn't have time for me."

"Well, she does now," Amy told him gently. "She wanted me to call you home tonight, even though she knew you would be angry."

"I wouldn't *be* angry if she didn't pull these stunts."

"Maybe it's the only way she knows how to get your attention."

He seemed to be chewing the inside of his cheek. "You think so?"

Amy followed her instincts. "Let me ask you something. Who keeps your house?"

"What?"

"Your house, who keeps it so neat and orderly? Who makes it so pleasant and comfortable?"

He actually had to think about it. "Well, we both do, I suppose. It just seems to kind of get done."

"It may just *seem* to get done," Amy pointed out, "but the truth is that someone has to be making that happen. I'd guess that someone is Mattie, but have you even noticed, Evans? You don't *seem* to."

He looked not just stunned but appalled. "You know, you're right. I never even thought of it." He thought of it now, leaning forward with both hands on the top rail. "It must have started as soon as her mother died. I was in a fog of grief and pain for a long time afterward, and I guess that by the time it cleared up… I remember being a little surprised that everything was running so smoothly. I guess I never stopped to think how or why."

"I think I'd dye my hair green, too," Amy suggested drolly.

His look was first derisive, then discerning. "You don't supposed she'll actually stop that once I shape up, do you?"

Amy laughed. "Don't underestimate what a little attention will do for a woman," she quipped, not realizing how appropriate those words were in her own case until she'd already said them. Suddenly she understood what was happening to her, why he bothered her so, why she felt…more alive than she had in a long time and ashamed at what she'd let herself come to. He had noticed her as a woman, and she liked it. She liked it very much, so much that it frightened her, especially when she realized that she hardly even thought of herself as a woman anymore. She'd all but killed everything womanly in her, buried it in the grave with Mark, and yet something about her had, miraculously, caught his attention, however slightly. She knew suddenly why she'd taken the time to wash her hair and put on a little makeup. She hadn't done that much before going out in public that afternoon! But in the middle of the night she'd slicked up to reprimand a teenager and confront her father! She was astounded at herself.

"Hey," he said, his hands skimming her upper arms lightly. "Don't go anywhere until I get back, will you? I want to speak with my daughter."

Amy nodded as much from the need to send him off as understanding. The moment he was gone she blanked her mind, afraid even to consider any longer why she was here. Before long she was regretting that capitulation. She wanted desperately to run home and slam the door, to lock out the Kincaids with the rest of the world. She wanted a cigarette, but when her lungs sucked in reflexively, they got clean, fresh air. Her head started spinning, and for a moment she felt disoriented, lost. Then Evans was back, incongruously apologizing for being gone so long.

"I really owe you a debt of thanks," he was saying. "I wish you could have seen her face when I complimented her on the job she's been doing around the house. I'm taking tomorrow evening off, God willing, and we're going to spend some quality time together, maybe take in a movie, talk. I—I've got to start opening my eyes to all she does around here, got to start *appreciating* her." He lifted a hand and rubbed the back of his neck. "Just how do you go about that, appreciating someone, I mean?"

Amy tried to pull her thoughts together. "Well…you start just like you said, you notice, and then…you show that you approve."

He nodded, smiling down at her. "I think I see what you mean. For instance, you did me a good turn tonight, handling this like you have."

She felt a shyness steal over her. "Oh, no, I didn't mean… that is, I wasn't thinking about anything I might have done."

"I am," he said softly, curling his hand beneath her chin when she meant to look down. "I appreciate what you've done, and I won't forget it."

"It was nothing," she muttered. "Now maybe I can listen to the TV at night."

He chuckled. "You're not as tough as you want people to think. In fact, you can be downright sweet when you want to be." He bent his head, his nose nearly brushing hers. "I appreciate that, too," he said, and then he laid his mouth over hers, keeping the touch feather light.

Amy was too stunned to react immediately, and before she could pull herself together to do so, it was all over, and he was smiling down at her again. She gulped, feeling flushed from head to toe, and quickly backed away. "I—I, um, have to go."

"Okay," he said. "See you."

"S-see you."

"Good night."

She all but ran. Once safely inside her own house, she leaned against the door and pulled a deep, calming breath through her nostrils, only to curl her nose at the musty, acrid odor that permeated the place. It was with equal parts dismay and delight that she realized there was no going back now. She was awake. The long, dark coma of grief had lifted, and it was time to live again.

Evans prodded Mattie determinedly, his tongue clamped behind his teeth to avoid haranguing her about her hair and makeup. *Where did she find these absurd shades? Where did one buy black lipstick?* He trusted Amy not to say anything that would get Mattie's back up. The last time he had dared to criticize her appearance, she had threatened to bleach that gorgeous black hair of hers. Sparkly hot pink highlights on bangs standing practically on end were not too much to bear when compared to bleach, and he could even stand the heavy eyeliner, but that black lipstick made him cringe every time he saw it. Nevertheless, he smiled and assured her that their next-door neighbor would be glad to see them. He hoped that he was right.

He hadn't so much as caught a glimpse of Amy since that night she'd called him home and so easily pointed out what was right under his nose—since the night he'd kissed her. He still couldn't quite believe he'd done that. Oh, she was attractive enough. In fact, her heart-shaped face was quite pretty with its big, bright blue eyes, little snip of a nose, and plump bow mouth. But Amy Slater just wasn't his type. He usually liked the lean, leggy sort, the sleek, fit, healthy kind he saw out running at daybreak. Yet, standing there on his front porch that night, listening to Amy's gentle explanation, he'd felt a compelling sense of rightness, a gentle contentment that had suddenly flared into physical need. He was glad he'd caught himself before he'd done something really stupid, something more than that light, almost friendly, kiss. He hoped that she hadn't realized that it might have been more. Ah, no, she wouldn't have done that, not when they'd fought almost every other time they'd met. Still, he felt it was his duty as her neighbor to keep an eye on her. She didn't really seem to have anyone else, even though she'd mentioned family. He'd just take Mattie along, even though Mattie wasn't as kindly disposed toward their only neighbor as he was, so Amy wouldn't get any farfetched ideas about his intentions.

He literally herded Mattie across their respective lawns. She grumbled every step of the way, but Evans ignored her with an almost confusing cheerfulness. It was only as he stood on Amy's front porch and knocked at her door that he began to feel misgivings. What if she slammed the door in their faces? She was fully capable of it. In fact, now that he thought about it, she was a strangely mercurial woman, shouting and scrabbling one minute, shy and quiet the next. She'd been patient and congenial and controlled the last time they'd met, but that didn't mean she would be so now. He almost turned around and hurried away, but suddenly the door was open and Amy was there, surprised pleasure flashing across her upturned face.

"Oh, hi! How are you guys?"

Evans felt himself grinning. "Fine! We're fine. How are you?"

"Oh, I'm all right. I'm...all right."

He nodded, absurdly pleased, while Mattie rolled her eyes at his side. Only the fear that she might say something rude prompted him to speak again. "We, ah, we hadn't seen you in a few days. We just wanted to check and be sure that everything's—you know—"

Amy laughed. Her face, alight with pleasure, was quite lovely. Evans felt his chest tighten, and his palms begin to sweat.

"Won't you come in?" she asked in a lilting voice.

He felt great relief, and only then realized that he'd feared she might not invite them in. He literally pushed Mattie through the door, whereupon she promptly wrinkled her nose and made a garish face.

"Ugh! It still smells."

His hand rested just inside her elbow. He tightened his grip warningly, appalled when she automatically yanked away.

"Will you behave yourself?" he hissed. "It's unbelievably rude to—"

"No," Amy injected, her hand falling on his forearm, "she's right. I realized it myself the other day. It's the cigarette odor. I couldn't smell it while I was smoking, but now…"

"Now your senses are no longer deadened by the smoke," he said. "Your senses are cleansing, and they're beginning to tell you what you've missed. That's great. That's really great."

"Yeah, if I can stick to it," she said.

His gaze fell on the coffee table and an open pack of cigarettes and a lighter there. He lifted an eyebrow. "Slipping a bit, are we?"

She shook her head and wrapped her arms around her middle. "Not that I haven't been tempted. I figure that as long as I can walk around them, I'm on the right track."

"You're still determined to quit then?" he asked softly.

She sucked a deep breath through her nostrils, her lips quirked up on one end, and she nodded emphatically.

He smiled. "Let's just lighten the load a bit then, shall we?"

She shrugged, and he bent to scoop up the cigarettes and lighter. His jeans were too tight to fit them in his pocket, so he simply lifted his T-shirt and tucked them behind the waistband of his pants. The look on Amy's face made him wonder if she was quite ready to let them go, but he didn't offer them back to her, and when she invited him and Mattie to have a seat, he considered the matter closed. Mattie sat down on the couch, and he dropped down next to her, stretching his arms out along its back. Amy took the chair opposite them and, drawing up a bare knee, linked her hands around it.

He noticed that the shorts she wore fit quite nicely and wondered if he'd seen her in them before. He couldn't really remember, and he didn't want to think about it. He didn't want to think about the way his heart was beating a little too quickly, either, or the twinge of victory he'd felt at tucking those cigarettes into his waistband. He was just being a good neighbor. That's all it was. And the sooner he forgot about that meaningless little kiss, the better.

Chapter Four

Her heart was thundering. She wondered if he could tell. He had to have noticed how her breath had seized and she'd had to drag her gaze away from his abdomen when he'd lifted his shirt. She couldn't think when she'd last seen a man's bare middle, but whenever it had been, it couldn't have hit her like the sight of his. The man was in excellent shape; she supposed he had to be, being a police officer. It occurred to her that she was stark raving mad to have entertained the idea, even momentarily, that he might be attracted to *her,* not that she'd really read anything into that brief, accidental kiss. Of course she hadn't.

She realized suddenly that Evans was talking, but when she forced her gaze to focus, she found herself looking at Mattie. Where on earth did the kid get that lipstick, not to mention the pink hair spray, and why was she pouting like a truculent toddler? Amy forced herself to concentrate on Evans. "I'm sorry. Would you repeat that?"

He looked momentarily pained, but then his face smoothed into a smile. "I said, I imagine you're wondering why we're here."

Amy made herself assume a pleasant expression. "Do neighbors need excuses to call on one another?"

"Uh, no. No, I don't suppose they do," he agreed.

Amy smiled. "Um, but you obviously do have a reason for coming over today."

Evans's smile faded slightly, but he sat forward and regarded her almost gravely. "I, um…" He paused and cleared his throat, but before Amy could offer him a glass of water, he went on. "Yes, we were wondering if you could recommend a local church to us."

"A church?"

Evans smiled and sat back, seemingly pleased with himself. "Yes, you see, we've visited a couple of places already, but we weren't completely comfortable. We just don't seem to have found where we belong yet, and we thought you might have some recommendation for us."

Amy felt absurdly out of her depth. A church? He wanted her to recommend a church? She hadn't been inside a church since the day she'd buried Mark. On the other hand, her sister Joan was very happy with her church. Amy licked her lips and tried not to feel hypocritical. "Um, well, Bolton Charles's church is a fine one. Even my brother-in-law regularly attends."

"Oh, that's right," Evans said, looking to Mattie. "I forgot to tell you. Guess who Amy's brother-in-law is?"

Mattie shrugged.

"Griff Shaw!" Evans announced. When she didn't seem to recognize the name, he added, "The bull rider."

Mattie said, "Oh," and nodded her head, but Amy could

tell that she didn't really know who Griff Shaw was. Evans, however, seemed suitably impressed.

"We'll certainly have to check it out," he said. "This Bolton Charles, he's your pastor?"

Amy couldn't help fidgeting slightly. "Uh, not *my* pastor, exactly."

"No?"

She felt a wave of embarrassment followed quickly by a flash of indignation. What business of his was it where or if she attended church? She had a right to her own convictions—or lack of them. She lifted her chin defensively. "I don't attend church anymore."

"Oh?" He cocked his head, and though his voice remained impassive, a flash of something very like disappointment came and went in his eyes. "You believe in God, don't you?"

"Certainly."

"Then perhaps you think Him unknowable?"

Her chin went up another notch. "Perhaps I do."

He nodded, and though she expected argument, he made none. Instead he said, "What about worship? I've always believed that worship is good for us. It certainly keeps me from believing that I am the center of the universe." He smiled self-deprecatingly, but Amy sensed another purpose beneath his queries. Something told her that this was important to him—and perhaps to her. She tried to give the matter serious thought, but the whole situation had her so flustered that she could not think beyond something she'd once heard Bolton Charles say. She seized it and made it her own.

"I do believe that God is worthy of worship," she said with satisfying dignity. "I just choose to worship in my own way."

"Ah," he said, "very commendable. Do you mind if I ask what you do, that is, how you worship?"

How? she thought, and of course there was no answer, for despite her statements, she had never really worshiped God on her own. But wasn't appreciation a form of worship? She had fairly often appreciated God's handiwork, such as a particularly lovely sunset, though *silently,* of course. In the same way she had occasionally given thanks, usually for escaping some accident or other. Surely everyone did that. She had even heard somewhere that unbelievers did it, too, that it was a sort of reflex, an *impersonal* thing. That couldn't rate very high with God. But then, what did she have for which to be personally thankful? Her husband had died a long, ugly death that a genuinely loving God would surely have prevented. *And yet,* her conscience said, *Evans Kincaid had lost his wife senselessly, and he was not bitter against God.* Bitter against God. Was she bitter against God? The very question disturbed her—and she blamed Evans. "I don't think my religion is any of your business," she said rather more sharply than she'd intended.

Was it her imagination or did his leaf green eyes seem to dull?

He nodded and politely said, "You're quite right. My apologies. Listen, I noticed recently that you seem to have some damage to the siding on your eaves. It's not very extensive yet, but you might want to start thinking about having them scraped and painted. Of course, you could wait and replace them. I just thought I'd mention it in case you preferred the cheaper route of prevention."

She seized gratefully upon the change of subject. "I— I'll have it looked at. Ah, th-thank you for bringing it to my attention."

He smiled perfunctorily. "What are neighbors for?"

"Oh. Yes. I agree. Neighbors really ought to…look out for one another."

"Exactly. Well," he said, sitting forward and sliding his hands down his thighs to his knees. "We have to be going now. Things to do. You know how it is."

"Yes, of course." She managed to get smoothly to her feet and smile at Mattie, who might have been somewhere else for all the attention she paid to what was being said and done around her. Evans had to reach down and catch her by the arm to make her realize that they were leaving. Then she leapt eagerly to her feet and made a smile for Amy.

"Well, goodbye!" she said brightly.

"Goodbye, Mattie." Inspiration struck, and Amy decided to follow her impulse for once. She took Mattie's hand. "Mattie, honey, if you should ever get—I don't know—lonely or bored at night when your dad's gone, why don't you just come on over? I'm pretty much a night person myself, and…well, it gets pretty lonely in the wee hours. And to tell you the truth, I'd rather have company than ruptured ear drums!"

Mattie's shock was obvious. "Really?"

"Absolutely."

Mattie laughed and looked to her father, who flashed his gaze over Amy then shrugged. Mattie beamed. "Okay! Sure."

"Great!" Amy said, realizing that she truly would welcome the company.

Evans was smiling, too, when he and Mattie took their leave. Amy found herself thinking that perhaps she had regained the esteem she had so recently lost in his eyes. Only then did she realize what she'd done—and why.

* * *

Mattie came over the very next evening. Amy was careful not to even mention Evans and to make only polite, meaningless comments whenever Mattie brought him up, which was too often for Amy's comfort. They watched an old movie together and resorted to making fun of it when it became obvious that Mattie was having a pretty hard time relating. All in all, it was a pleasant evening, and Amy felt that she just might have made a friend by the time Mattie fell asleep on the couch. When daylight dawned and Evans came dragging home, Amy woke Mattie and sent her out to meet him. He looked in Amy's direction and lifted his hand in a wave after greeting his daughter with an arm slung about her shoulders, but he did not come over or speak. Amy told herself that it was for the best as she readied herself for bed, but she couldn't help feeling disappointed.

The feeling stayed with her until an afternoon several days later, when the dull rumble of a mower reached beyond the gentle hum of the central air-conditioning and into the shallows of an uneasy slumber, bringing a name to her mind. Evans. Evans Kincaid. Evans Kincaid was mowing his yard. Evans Kincaid was mowing his yard in the heat of the day. Facedown, she mentally shook her head at his gluttony for punishment and let herself drift in that comfortable place between wakefulness and real sleep—until the rumble grew louder and somehow measured, prompting new thought: Evans Kincaid was mowing *her* yard in the heat of the day. The dear.

Amy rolled over, groaning as she realized just where her thoughts were taking her. But it was true. Her yard needed mowing. Evans was undoubtedly doing it, and it was very sweet of him to do so. He was a good neighbor, a better neighbor than she. He was, in fact, a better *person* than she. He had lost his wife, the mother of his child, but he hadn't let himself and everything around him go to pot, and he didn't resent God for taking the woman he loved. Amy stared up at the dingy ceiling of her bedroom and told herself that things were going to change, starting now.

Sitting up, she threw her legs over the side of the bed, stretched her arms, shoulders and spine, then stood. What, she wondered, could she do for him? What neighborly thing would show her appreciation? In this hot weather, he was bound to appreciate something cold to drink. The fact that it was a rather obvious solution deterred her not at all. She moved briskly toward the kitchen to put on a fresh pot of tea to steep. On the way, she caught a glimpse of herself in the dresser mirror and shuddered. While the tea was steeping, she was going to pull herself together.

She did just that. After catching a quick shower, she mixed the tea and placed it in the refrigerator to chill. Then she quickly blew her hair dry at the roots in order to fluff it up some. By the time she had applied a bit of light makeup to her face, darkened her brows and eyelashes, her hair was curling attractively about her face. She changed her sleep shirt for a cotton knit short set of coral pink and traded her sandals for a pair of simple white canvas shoes. Next she filled a quart jar with ice cubes and unsweetened tea.

He had traded the mower for an edger and was grooming the borders of the sidewalk next to the street. He was wearing cutoffs and tennis shoes, his shirt hanging from his back pocket, an obvious concession to the heat. Nevertheless, his lean, sun-browned torso glistened with perspiration. It was a sight to make Amy catch her breath and swallow it, but she kept her expression determinedly relaxed as she carried the iced tea across the yard. He stopped what he was doing and mopped his brow with his shirt as she drew near. His smile was absolutely blinding even before he spotted the tea. She was surprised by how much that pleased her.

"Thought you might like this," she said, handing over the quart jar. "Tea, not syrup, this time."

He laughed at that before taking a long swallow of the cold beverage. "Ahhhhhh." He rubbed the cold jar over his face and throat. "Wonderful." His smile renewed itself. "Thanks."

"Thank *you*," she countered. "You didn't have to mow my yard, you know. I have a boy who comes around to do it from time to time, when he needs money, I expect."

He shrugged. "I was doing mine. I figured that while I had the mower out, I might as well cut everything that needed cutting. Besides, I like the looks of this neighborhood when all the yards are done. It makes me think of a green, manicured oasis in the middle of all this brown heat."

Amy glanced around her, noticing for the first time how green her yard looked. "That's odd," she said. "Things are usually all burned up around here by now."

He swallowed another long drink of tea and lowered the jar. "I, um, I've been watering it when I water my own. And I figure if I'm making it grow, I ought to keep it groomed."

She was surprised but not displeased, which she should have been, considering his high-handedness. But things were not as simple as that any longer. She even thought a little wistfully about the shield of anger that she might have wrapped herself in only days ago. But it was gone now. She wasn't sure how or why, only that when she reached for it, it wasn't there.

She squinted up at Evans, wondering what he'd done to her. "Making that green, manicured oasis happen, you mean?"

He grinned. "Something like that, but with some good old neighborly concern thrown in."

She nodded and looked away, uncertain what to say or do next. The obvious would have to do again. "It looks good, real good."

"So do you," he said lightly, lifting his jar once more.

She tried not to blush and fought a feeling of such pleasure that it was frightening. She couldn't just ignore such a compliment, however. She licked suddenly dry lips. "Why, thank you."

He lowered the jar, his gaze suddenly keen. "You're welcome. I thought you might like to know that somebody had noticed. When you live alone, there's nobody to notice but you, so it's real easy to let things slide. It helps when somebody else notices you've put out some effort."

Boy, did he ever hit that nail on the head! And the truth was that she was glad he had noticed. It occurred to her then that he had made her care again. Somehow, he had made it matter if she left her house looking like she'd just crawled up out of a hard night or looking her best. Maybe it was time to start caring about more than herself, too. She took a deep breath and, not quite meeting his gaze, confessed, "I've let a lot slide around here. I think it's time I started putting out some effort again. Where better to start than with me?"

He chuckled. "True."

She smiled, then sighed. "The problem is, I've let a lot more go than I can correct with just my own effort. I was wondering, would you mind if I asked Mattie to help me clean my house during this last week before school starts? I'd pay her, of course, and…well, she certainly seems to know her way around a mop and pail."

"She does that," he agreed proudly, and drained the last of his tea. "I certainly don't mind if you ask her," he said thoughtfully, "but I can't say for sure how she'll answer you."

"We'll leave it up to her then," Amy said with satisfaction.

"I hope she does it," he said softly. "I think it'd be good for her. It's been a long time since she enjoyed the company of a woman."

"She must miss her mother terribly," Amy said.

He nodded. "I'm sure she does, but it's more than that with Mattie, too. I wish I understood it."

"Who really understands kids?" Amy asked lightly.

He locked his gaze with hers. "You understood that she was lonely," he said, "that she needed me to acknowledge and appreciate all the good she does. You understood that she still needs me, when all I could see was the crazy hair and the rebelliousness."

"They say rebelliousness is just part of growing up, a way to move from childhood to adulthood."

"And the weird hairdos and makeup?" he asked.

She shrugged. "Maybe she's just trying to find herself, you know? Figure out who the real Mattie is."

He shook his head, grinning. "Well, if that's the case, I hope the *real* Mattie's a little more conservative."

She laughed. "Maybe I can nudge her in that direction."

"I'd be eternally grateful," he quipped. "You'd probably get your yard mowed for the rest of your life, not to mention some general repairs and maintenance around the place."

It was hot, and Amy could feel the perspiration beginning to trickle down the canal of her spine. Besides, she was keeping him from finishing up and getting inside where it was cool. She took the empty jar from him and tossed out the ice. "Let's see what success I have first," she said, backing away. "Thanks again."

"You're welcome again," he said, nodding and bending toward the edger once more.

As he started it up, she turned and walked into the house, smiling.

Mattie agreed to help Amy clean and reorganize her house, but "only for the money," or so she said. The girl possessed an amazing work ethic, however. The very day after Amy spoke to her, Mattie showed up at Amy's house bright and early with every imaginable cleaning aid in tow. It took five minutes to move it all into the house. Amy had unwisely stayed up all night the night before and was not in the best of moods, but Mattie bullied her into acceptance with nothing more than a determinedly cheerful attitude and a deaf ear. And she was nothing if not organized in her approach. She literally canvased the house, poking her nose into every closet, cabinet and drawer. She even looked under the beds, and declared that everything there had to go—especially the dust bunnies! She went so far as to write down on paper everything that had to be done, providing them with a checklist three notebook pages long!

Amy would have had an easier time accepting Mattie's instruction if it hadn't been for the girl's bizarre appearance. For one thing, she was wearing solid black: shorts, T-shirt, socks and high-top shoes, but that was the least of it. Mattie had twisted up her long, straight hair so that it lay smoothly against her head everywhere except in front and right on top.

These two sections she had ratted and pulled out at strange angles, some to droop about her face, some to stand on end, and she had sprayed the whole of it a veritable rainbow of glow-in-the-dark colors. In addition, she had painted her eyelids white and applied a layer of ultra shiny bloodred lip gloss. The effect was positively garish, especially as she kept cracking the gum that she was chewing.

Amy longed to order the girl home for a good scrubbing, but she knew that making an issue of her appearance was the surest way to guarantee that she wouldn't change it. Her own experience as a teenager had taught her that. In fact, she vividly recalled an episode over a white halter top that her parents had criticized as being too skimpy for modesty. For weeks she'd worn it at every available opportunity, going so far as to sneak out of the house with it on under other clothes. Only when her friends had begun to complain about seeing her in the same thing all the time had she stopped wearing it in public, but even then she'd worn it around the house just to steam her parents. When they finally stopped complaining, she'd gotten sick of the thing herself pretty quickly. Later, she couldn't even remember why she'd liked it in the first place!

So Amy said nothing about Mattie's outrageous appearance. She pushed away her own reluctance and even ignored the physical exhaustion with which she'd awakened, finding strength in a pot of strong, black coffee while Mattie was organizing her checklist. It was the lull before the storm, so to speak, because she quickly found herself wielding broom and feather duster and vacuum wand with more desperation than enthusiasm as Mattie began to tear apart her house.

Amy fell into bed that first night in a stupor of exhaustion, confusion and dismay. The house was a wreck, the contents of every closet, drawer and cupboard pulled out onto the floor and furniture, while said closets, drawers and cupboards were cleaned from the topmost corners to the very bottoms. The drapes had been pulled down from the windows and sent out for cleaning, along with a mountain of bed coverings. Linens and curtain sheers went into the washing machine, which itself was given a thorough cleaning, then were hung on the Kincaids' clothesline to dry in the sun.

Every throw rug in the place wound up on the porch, where they were hosed down, sprinkled with laundry detergent, scrubbed with a broom and hosed down again before being thrown over the fence in the backyard to dry. Light fixtures came down off ceilings and were soaked in a mixture of vinegar, water and detergent. Lamp shades were vacuumed, dusted with talc and vacuumed again, and then the procedure was repeated until each and every shade looked brand new. Baseboards, windowsills, window casings and door facings had been dusted, scrubbed with special wood soap and oiled to a bright sheen. The same process, Mattie had informed her, would be used later on every piece of furniture in the house. First, however, they would go through Amy's possessions item by item in order to decide what had outlived its usefulness and must be discarded.

Mattie was true to her word. The very next day she made sure that Amy, though stiff and sore, was at her side while she examined and questioned every effect that Amy had accumulated over the years. If it was not for emergency or special use, or if Amy had not used it within the last year or acquired it under unusually sentimental circumstances, it went into one of two piles, either designated for charity or the trash. Everything else was cleaned, organized and readied for storage, so that in the end, everything had its place and was in it. The organization of it was all Mattie's, and Amy marveled at the ease with which she put it all together in the most logical, workable fashion. The sense of it was blatant, and yet Amy herself had not thought to arrange her belongings in such a manner. Mattie proposed to tape labels to all the shelves and drawers in order to help Amy become familiar with the new system, especially in the kitchen, but Amy did not find it necessary, the logic of Mattie's plan was that firm.

They called a halt early that evening, but Amy was so tired from the exertions of the past two days that she went to bed without dinner and slept soundly through the night. When Mattie arrived bright and early the next morning, garbed all in lime green and her hair sprayed to match, Amy was ready and waiting for her, a cup of coffee in hand and a smile on her face, despite the aching muscles that occasionally produced winces.

It was the hardest day yet. By nightfall, the walls and ceilings in every room had been swept and washed; the floors were given the additional benefit of a good waxing. The carpets were vacuumed and shampooed. The windows were polished inside and out. The countertops and bathroom fixtures were scrubbed and bleached to a dazzling white. Not even the laundry hamper escaped sanitizing. And the furniture…

Mattie insisted that every upholstered piece had to be carried outside and beaten to loosen the dirt, which was then vacuumed repeatedly and carried back inside to be shampooed by hand and vacuumed again once it was dry. The wood portions were scrubbed with special soap and an old toothbrush where there was carving, then polished dry with a soft cloth, oiled, and polished again until the wood gleamed.

Knobs and handles were given the same treatment. Finally, casters and rollers were cleaned with bottle brushes dipped in alcohol, then lubricated for easy movement. By the time it was all cleaned and rearranged, Amy could have slept standing up against the wall—if she hadn't been afraid of leaving a smudge that Mattie would have ordered immediately cleaned.

Nevertheless, by day four, Amy found her enthusiasm burgeoning rather than diminishing. The house smelled like heaven and was organized to perfection. Wood gleamed. Glass glittered. The whole place felt lighter, brighter. The draperies, bedspreads, and blankets returned from the cleaners and again covered windows and beds. Whatnots, pictures and books were cleaned and placed in pleasing new arrangements, and finally, every remaining appliance, small or large, was dismantled so far as practical and cleaned to within an inch of its existence, including refrigerator, stove, microwave, toaster, dryer, coffee maker, oven and so on. Even the central air unit and the hot water heater received Mattie's expert ministrations.

Amy stood in awe of her young friend's gift for homemaking. Mattie herself spoke often of her desire for a home and family of her own, so that Amy came to understand that it was family more than anything else that Mattie craved. She missed her mother, but Amy was impressed by how easily and fondly Mattie recalled her deceased parent. Mattie had grieved, yes, but the sheer joy of that relationship so completely overshone the pain of loss itself that Amy was forced to reevaluate her own experience. It occurred to her that there might have been less true joy in her marriage than she had believed, even before the onset of her husband's illness. She had fashioned herself as much as possible to his desires without regard for her own wishes or inclinations—and he had let her; he had, in fact, *required* that she do so. Yet, somehow she had not quite managed to truly please him on many occasions. She did not come to these conclusions without suffering a heavy dose of guilt, but guilt was an all-too-familiar emotion for Amy, and she suffered it with practiced stoicism.

Mattie was a constant diversion, however, and as the two worked side by side, Amy came to understand that Mattie's need for family was predicated upon her sense that she was out-growing her role as Daddy's little girl. At one and the same time, she resented and treasured her place in his heart and home. More to the point, she understood at some deep emotional level that they both needed more than each other; yet, she hadn't the least idea where that something more might be found. Put suc-cinctly, Mattie was a girl poised on the threshold of woman-hood, longing for the one man in the world who could join with her in creating the kind of family that her own mother and father had made together. But not even Mattie knew it, and Amy doubted very much that Evans Kincaid wanted to hear it.

Yet, Amy knew that Mattie was at a very vulnerable place. It was a place that Amy recognized without ever consciously admitting that she, too, had dwelled there. It was a place from which Amy knew with awful certainty that Mattie could be lured with dangerous ease by the wrong man. Amy did not want to think that this disquieting knowledge came from personal experience, but just because Amy didn't want to think it, didn't mean it wasn't so. And just because Amy could close her mind to this startling insight didn't mean that she could avoid having her insides worked over as surely as her outside surroundings, so that by the time her house was all rearranged and polished, so were her moods and emotions.

It would never again seem normal or preferable to close her door on the outside world and closet herself alone with her grief and her guilt and her anger. The long dark night was over, and never again could she lock out the day. It was as if she'd embarked upon a journey and wouldn't even know where she was going until she got there. The prospect was both exciting and terrifying, and the only certainty was that she couldn't go back even if she'd wanted to, which she didn't. That in itself was the most shocking aspect of the whole situation. For the first time in a long time, she actually did not want to go back.

Chapter Five

"Hungry?"

Amy and Mattie looked up from the floor. Mattie was folding the last freshly laundered load of bath towels. Amy was merely trying to gather the strength to get up and walk to the shower. She shielded her eyes from the glare of a sparkling clean overhead light fixture and studied him. He looked as fresh and fragrant as the towels that Mattie was folding. His bright blue T-shirt hugged his muscular torso like a second skin, its hem disappearing behind the snug waistband of dark, crisp jeans. His inky hair had been brushed back from his forehead. His bronzed jaw looked freshly shaved. His smile was dazzlingly white. She couldn't tell for certain, but she suspected that his yellow-green eyes glinted with humor, and she suspected that he was silently laughing at her. She couldn't blame him.

She knew that she must look a sight, her hair and clothing

plastered to her with sweat, her face slack with exhaustion, her body stiff with soreness. In fact, she imagined that she and Mattie together were as bizarre a pair as could be seen in town. She imagined them as they must look, she worn to a frazzle, Mattie decked out from her spiked head to her toes in fluorescent lime green, and suddenly laughter was bubbling up. It started, really, as a wiggly grin, then became chuckles and sputters and, as the others began to join in, hard, erupting guffaws.

"What?" Evans kept saying. "What'd I say?"

Laughter gave Amy the energy to shake her head and sit up. "No, no, it wasn't you. I mean, look at us, a drowned r-rat and a p-p-peacock!" She flipped her hand upward from her brow, copying Mattie's "plume."

Mattie gasped, then aimed a playful slap at Amy's leg. "I do not look like a peacock!"

"You're right," Evans said, his solemn tone completely spoiled by the sputters of fresh laughter. "M-more like a p-parrot!"

"Da-ad!"

"And Amy!" he gasped, doubling over. "What'd you do to her? Use her to clean the bathtub?"

Amy caught a picture of herself slithering around inside the tub while Mattie sprinkled a cloud of scouring powder over her and went off in fresh gales of uncontrollable mirth. Mattie must have gotten a glimpse of the same scene for she suddenly clamped both hands over her mouth and collapsed at Amy's side. They rolled around on the floor for several minutes, howling, while Evans crouched before them and shook his head. After some time, the humor began to fade. Mattie sat up and wiped her eyes, smearing kohl over her cheeks. "Ahem, I think it's the ammonia fumes," she said seriously enough to set Amy off again.

It was only seconds before the laughter receded this time and Amy was able to sit up and add her theory to the mix. "It's exhaustion, pure exhaustion." She sighed with the passing of the hilarity and wiped her own eyes with grimy hands.

"I think you're both delirious with hunger," Evans pronounced wryly, "which is precisely why I'm marinating chicken breasts for the grill. What do you say to that with a tossed green salad and steamed corn on the cob?"

"Are you inviting me to dinner?" Amy asked, thoroughly surprised.

He canted his head, grinning. "You're not as tired as you look. Yes, I am inviting you to dinner."

The comment about her looks, while suggesting nothing she didn't already know, produced a certain insecurity that sent a hand to her hair. She dropped it at once. What did she care, anyway? He was just her next-door neighbor, after all, an acquaintance, a casual friend. He tilted his head in the opposite direction.

"Well? What do you say? Want to take a chance on my cooking or not?"

"He's a good cook," Mattie said, "at least when it comes to the grill."

"Hey!" Evans objected. "I can steam an ear of corn."

Mattie rolled her eyes and looked at Amy. "We have an electric steamer. You just pour the water in and turn it on."

Amy grinned mischievously. "And what about the salad?"

"Ready-made," Mattie confided dryly.

"Well, I put the chicken in marinade," Evans insisted.

"Bottled," Mattie said succinctly.

Evans threw up his hands. "I give up! This is the thanks I get for using my night off to provide sustenance for the two of you."

"Your night off you say?" Amy chirped. "Well, that's different." She elbowed Mattie to clue her into the joke, and Mattie caught on at once.

"Oh, he's a much better cook on his night off," she said.

Evans pushed up to his full height and aimed a pretend glare down at the two of them, his hands on his hips. "Oh, you're too cute. Chicken goes on in ten minutes, and twelve minutes after that, I eat."

"Twenty-two minutes!" Mattie exclaimed. "That's not enough time to shower and get ready. We have to wash and fix our hair and—"

Amy gritted her teeth and bounced up to her feet. "We'll be there," she said. "Thanks."

Evans's grin was quick. "You're welcome." He pointed a finger at Mattie. "Twenty-two minutes."

Amy was headed for the shower before he got through the front door. Mattie went into a panic. "Amy, help me finish these towels!"

"Leave 'em!" she called, wrenching on the water. "I'll finish them later."

"A-my!" Mattie protested.

Amy went back to the bathroom door and stuck her head out while she shucked her shorts. "You heard him," she shouted, peering down the hall. "Twenty-one minutes and counting."

Mattie made a frustrated sound and continued folding towels, hands flying. "I hate to leave things undone!"

Amy ignored her and ripped her T-shirt over her head. In two seconds she'd stripped off both panties and bra and was stepping behind the plastic curtain into the tub. When she stepped out spare minutes later and wrapped herself in a towel, she was amazingly rejuvenated. A quick check revealed that Mattie had gone. The towels were folded and stacked on the living room floor. Amy smiled at that. The kid was just a tad obsessive, but Amy couldn't deny that she had benefited greatly from Mattie's preoccupation with cleanliness and order. She decided to do something extra nice for her, a bonus of sorts. Maybe she'd give herself a bonus, too. Heaven knew she'd worked harder these past few days than ever before in her life.

Her stomach growled as she toweled her hair, reminding her to hurry. She ran to the bedroom, ripped underclothes from their drawers and jeans from their hanger and jumped into them. Was it her imagination or were these jeans a little roomier than before? She shrugged and threw on a collarless gold silk blouse with short sleeves and buttons up the front. She put her bare feet into tan, fringed flats, slipped on her watch, and hurried back to the bathroom to take a dryer to her hair and apply some light makeup, including clove-colored lipstick and fawn brown eye shadow. Her hair didn't seem to want to cooperate, so she dried it a little more and whipped a brush through it until it crackled and flowed away from her face in gentle, fluffy waves. A glance at her watch told her that she was running a minute behind. She ran out, leaving all the lights on and the door unlocked.

She went straight to the Kincaids' backyard and found Evans there turning chicken breasts over a gas grill with a long, gleaming fork. "Smells great."

He turned and flashed her a smile. His eyes went wide and his brows sprang up. "Well, look at you! No more drowned rats around here, I see."

She wrinkled her nose, feeling conspicuous and not the least unhappy about it. "I know I looked really awful. Some women, like my sister, Joan, manage to perspire prettily. I, on the other hand, sweat like a pig."

He laughed and said, "Well, you'd never know it to look at you now."

She looked down at herself. "Thanks. I think I've even lost a little weight. Oh, well, I'll probably gain it right back."

He sent her a look over his shoulder. "I don't see why. Exercise seems to agree with you. Why not keep it up?"

She shrugged wryly. "What would you suggest? That I sweep and mop the street four or five times a week?"

He laughed again. "Nothing so productive. Why not do what I do and run three or four times a week?"

She pondered that a moment, wondering if he was inviting her along on his runs. "I might," she said finally.

That seemed to satisfy him. He took up a small platter from a wheeled metal table at his side and forked the three chicken breasts onto it. "I thought we'd eat inside," he said, shoving the platter at her. "It's still pretty warm out."

"Suits me," she replied, turning toward the house.

He cut off the gas and locked down the hood of the grill, then quickly gathered up the fork and a kitchen towel from the table and followed after Amy. He was right on her heels by the time she came to the door, and he reached around her to open it for her. In doing so, his chest bumped her back. The touch so jolted her that she bobbled the platter. His arms came around her, fork, towel and all, as he attempted to steady the plate. An unfamiliar mix of emotion and sensation flashed over her, both mesmerizing and paralyzing.

It was as if she felt him in every cell of her body, and for a long moment she could do nothing *but* feel. Then Evans dropped the towel and brought his arm snug against her, his hand splayed across her midriff. Sensation as red-hot as the iron briquettes in the gas grill jolted her into sudden action. She jerked away, the platter all but hugged to her chest, and stumbled into the kitchen. Evans's hand clamped down on her arm and turned her toward him. From the look of incredulity on his face, she knew that he was as stunned by that brief connection as she was.

"Amy?" he rasped, that one word becoming a loaded question.

Mattie ricocheted into the room, her chatter muffled by the towel she was in the process of wrapping around her head. "Best I can do," she was saying. "When you don't give a person time to catch her breath, you get— Why, Amy! It certainly doesn't take you long to get it together." She put a hand on her hip, the little jumper she was wearing hitching well up her thigh. "You ever think of dying your hair? You know, adding a little drama to the package?"

Evans released Amy abruptly. "Don't be silly, Matilda," he snapped. "There's nothing wrong with Amy's hair." He turned away and moved to the counter. "I thought we'd eat in the kitchen. Anybody mind? Get the salad out of the fridge, Mattie, and don't forget the dressing. Pick a chair, Amy, and put the platter on the table."

She did exactly as instructed, moving as if by rote. Her mouth was too dry to speak, her heart still pounding wildly in her chest. She thought inanely that she ought to run home, that it was dangerous for her to be here, but she didn't want to run. She didn't want to hide. For once, she wanted to be part of the game. She wanted to be right here. She wanted to belong, and if her heart was pounding, it was because the feeling was so new and because she was exhausted. It was a pleasant exhaustion, though, the exhaustion of accomplishment, of new beginnings already begun. She pushed the unnamed fears away and relaxed, laughing as Mattie teased Evans about his cooking skills. Soon she was enjoying herself immensely, that haunting moment of electric awareness safely filed away in the very back of her mind.

Evans smiled at Amy and pushed his plate away. He'd thought for a time that she was going to bolt, but then Mattie had started to jabber and he'd felt Amy relax. He was glad, more glad than he wanted to be. But he wasn't one to fight the inevitable. He'd felt this coming for some time. More and more, lately, he'd found himself contemplating the widow Slater and what it would take to get under that prickly exterior to the soft heart that he suspected she protected beneath it. He told himself as they laughed over dinner that perhaps they had been waiting for each other without even knowing it. He didn't think he was wrong in suspecting that the loss of her husband was a wound only freshly healed, despite the time that had passed. If he had believed in coincidence, he might have said it was a trick of fate that had brought him here, but his faith in God left no room for fate or mere happenstance. Was this the woman God had sent him in answer to his repeated prayers? He thought wryly that perhaps he ought to have asked for a woman with a less complicated emotional makeup, but then he remembered something that Andie had told him.

A man, she had said, might assign only a part of his emotional strength to love and consider that his all, reserving the remainder of his devotion for things and events, accomplishments and pleasures;

but a woman loved with the true weight of her emotions whether she wanted to or not. She had told him, too, how glad she was that he held nothing back, for a woman like herself, who loved with a depth and breadth of emotion frightening in its scope, would live in hell with a man who could not or would not give back the same intensity of feeling. Without that emotional sustenance, Andie had insisted, such a woman would wither and die inside. Might not the same thing happen to a very emotional woman, he wondered, without anyone to love? That being so, he asked himself, which case applied to Amy?

The next moment he told himself it didn't matter. He had no doubt that she had been deeply wounded, that she had withdrawn into herself. The exact cause didn't seem important. What mattered was that he could help her open her heart to love again. He was suddenly sure of it. He didn't stop to think that in prying open Amy's heart, he was opening himself to a sort of pain he had never before, in any substantive way, felt—the pain of rejection.

It was Mattie's yawn that told him the evening should be brought to a swift conclusion. He smiled at her with the kind of fondness he too often failed to show. She looked like a little girl tonight with her face washed clean and her hair soft and shiny black. This was who she really was. He stifled the urge to tuck her into bed and said instead, "Why don't you turn in, Mattie-girl? You must be tired to the bone."

She shook her head wearily. "I'll just help you clean up first."

She reached for a plate, but he snatched it out of her hand. "I'll take care of this as soon as I take care of the two of you.

Now, I want you to get to bed while I walk Amy home. Don't worry, I'll clean up the kitchen as soon as I get back. Okay?"

"Okay, Dad." She got up, went around the table, and kissed him on the cheek. "Good night."

"Good night, babe."

"Good night, Mattie," Amy said.

She left the room on another yawn, making both Amy and Evans chuckle. Amy shook her head fondly. "She has been an invaluable help to me, a dictator, but invaluable."

"I guess that's one trait she inherited from me," he admitted sheepishly.

"Well, you can add meticulousness to the list," she informed him smartly.

He put his elbows on the table and ran his fingers through his hair. "Is this list going to be a long one?"

She smiled. "I'll let you know."

He smiled back. "You do that."

He tried to hold her gaze, to tell her without words that he was glad to know she had granted them some sort of future, but she dropped her head, and if he wasn't mistaken, actually blushed. Suddenly she bolted from her chair. "I'd better be getting home."

"I'll walk you," he said, coming to his feet.

"No, you don't have—"

"I'll walk you." Instinctively he had imbued his voice with the tone of command.

She looked up sharply, one delicate brow cocked in obstinate denial. For an instant, mischief sparkled in those bright blue eyes, but then something far more cautious chased it away, and she jerked her gaze from his, nodding in acquiescence. She moved quickly toward the door, but he caught up with her on the porch, skipped the steps and was waiting for her as she descended.

He caught up her hand and wrapped it around his forearm, holding her close to his side. As before, awareness tingled between them, but he followed her lead and ignored it as they strolled across his yard, out his gate and along the back of his garage to a small break in the hedges that marked the boundary of Amy's property. He followed her through the space in the shrubbery, his hand sliding down her arm then dropping to her waist as he joined her on the other side.

"Thank you," she said simply as they drew near the small back stoop that led into her kitchen.

"For what?" he teased silkily. "For walking you home? For dinner? For loaning you my daughter?"

"All three," she said lightly, "and every other kind, caring thing you've done."

"I don't want thanks," he told her in a near whisper.

"Well, you have it, anyway."

"I'd rather have this," he said, halting and drawing her to him. His hands lit on her shoulders, then skimmed up her throat to cup her face, tilting it slightly before his mouth came down over hers.

The jolt of electricity that he felt as their mouths blended nearly knocked him off his feet. He swayed and moaned, instinctively deepening the kiss, his arms dropping about her as his tongue slid into her mouth. Her hands crept around his waist, and he felt the heat in his groin that marked the rush of blood that came with arousal. He stepped closer, drew her tighter against him, enveloped himself in the velvet of her mouth. Only when she wrenched away did he realize that she had been pulling back for some moments, her hands wedged against his chest. He released her at once, stunned by this turn.

"How dare you!" she said, her chest heaving with gasps of breath.

He had to close his mouth and swallow before he could speak. "Amy, I—"

"I don't want to be pawed and kissed, not by anyone, and certainly not by you!" she cried.

Icy cold swept him and then white-hot anger. "I apologize," he said stiffly and turned on his heel.

"Damn you!" he heard her sob behind him. "Why can't you leave me alone? Just leave me alone!"

"Oh, I will!" he vowed. He felt as if she had slapped him. Rejection stung straight to his heart. He was in his own yard before the blinding mist of pain and anger lifted enough to let him take note of his surroundings. He sat on the top step of his porch and hung his head between his hands.

What had made him think that that woman could offer him anything but grief? How could he entertain the notion, even for a moment, that he might be what she needed and vice versa? Why had he made such a fool of himself over her? He shook his head, shocked at the depth of bitterness he was feeling. Well, he wouldn't make that mistake again! And from now on, Widow Slater could mow her own yard and do everything else that needed doing! He would tend to his own house—and his own heart.

Amy slammed the door and leaned against it. Dear God, what had she done? How could she have let him kiss her, let alone kiss him back? She imagined Mark glaring down at her from heaven, disgust and condemnation on his face. Guilt literally shoved her into a chair at the kitchen table, bent her double and sent tears coursing down her face. How could this be happening to her? What on earth did she think she was doing? Her life did not need to be changed. She was a widow. Her husband was dead. She could never love again. She could never…what? She lifted her head. Be happy? Was that her lot in life, to be miserably unhappy for all the lonely years ahead? Was that what Mark had meant for her? Was that what she deserved?

You were a good wife, she told herself. *You were loyal. You believed in him. No matter what he did or said, you made yourself believe!* And for that she had only her guilt to keep her company.

But it was not her fault that the illness had come! It was not her fault that he had died! Why hadn't God cured the disease and let Mark live? He was all she'd had, after all. But was he all she could ever have? All she should have?

She didn't know anymore. She only knew that Evans Kincaid terrified her. He made her wonder if what she'd dedicated herself to, what she'd grieved all this time, had been worth the loyalty and love with which she'd lavished it.

She shook her head, desperate tears welling into her eyes. How could she think it? How could she? Oh, God, how could she?

The grass grew tall in Amy's yard, then burned brown in the sun and dwindled to scraggly spikes. Evans made himself ignore it, as he ignored her, as he ignored Mattie's every word about the goings-on next door.

"She's stopped smoking again," Mattie told him brightly the day after school began. "I told her she was stinking up her house and I wasn't about to help her clean it up this time."

Evans polished the wrench he had used to make an adjustment to the dishwasher and slipped it into its sleeve. "Let me know if it starts making that droning sound again."

Mattie waved a hand dismissively and popped a potato chip into her mouth. She curled her legs up into her chair and munched the chip, her heavily kohled eyes narrowed.

"Anyway, she's so weird, right now. It's like she doesn't know what to do with herself. I think she's lost some weight. Maybe she's depressed, I don't know. What do you think?"

He wiped his hands on a towel and got to his feet. "How was school?"

She made a face and shrugged. "It's not as lame as California, but it's still, you know, lame."

Evans sighed. "Why don't you give it a chance, try to fit in a little more?"

"I don't want to fit in. Ugh, why would I want to fit in? They're babies."

Evans sat down at the table and leaned against his forearms. "They're your age, Mattie. Are you saying they're less mature than you?"

"I don't know. I guess. They just seem like…babies."

Evans felt terribly confused and inadequate, and the feeling made him angry again—at Amy. He couldn't seem to separate his feelings from Amy. But he darn well would. He swallowed the anger and focused on his daughter. "I think you may have grown up faster than most kids in some ways," he said carefully, "but that doesn't make you an adult, honey."

Mattie swiped her hair back off her shoulder angrily. "What does make me an adult? Just age? Amy says it's more than that. Amy says…"

"Amy doesn't have anything to do with this!" Evans shouted, smacking the tabletop with his hand.

Mattie was obviously shocked. "All I said was—"

"I know, I know," he muttered angrily, bowing his head. He closed his eyes, willing away his anger, and took a deep breath before saying, "I just don't think Amy is the person to be giving you advice."

"At least Amy doesn't think I'm a baby!" Mattie retorted, springing to her feet.

Evans kept his head down, praying for patience. "I didn't say you were a baby," he told her calmly. "I only said that you aren't yet completely an adult. I only suggested that since you *have* to go to school, you might be happier if you tried to fit in. Now could we drop the subject, *please?*"

Mattie sat down again, her upper teeth worrying her bottom lip. "I've been thinking about something, and maybe now's the time to talk about it."

Evans spread his hands in a gesture of compliance, relieved that she was actually going to take his advice about *something.* "What's on your mind, hon?"

Mattie chewed her lip a moment longer. "I was thinking, maybe I ought to get a part-time job of some sort."

Evans tilted his head. "I suppose, if that's what you want."

She suddenly became animated, excited. "It'd give me something to do besides going to school and waiting for you to come home from work, and I'd have my own spending money! You wouldn't have to give me any more."

Evans rubbed his chin speculatively. "Hmm, and what would you do with your money?"

She shrugged entirely too nonchalantly. "Oh, I don't know, the usual kind of stuff, clothes, makeup, music…a car."

Red flags immediately went up. A car, was it? Evans thought quickly. With a car of her own, she would pretty much be free to come and go as she wished when he was not around. He wasn't sure she was mature enough for that kind of freedom. She could go anywhere, do just about anything, even strike out across the country for California and that rock freak they'd left behind! His blood ran cold, and his mind immediately conjured more justifications for refusal. What about accidents? Some of the car wrecks he'd seen were enough to make a sober man take up walking for life. To think of his little girl wrapped around some telephone pole somewhere... He shuddered and emerged from it shaking his head.

"No. Not a good idea. No. Uh-uh. No way. You're too young for a car."

"But Dad—"

"No! I'm not going to lose you to some mindless accident like I did your mother! Too many teenagers die in cars, Matilda. I'm not going through that!"

"You don't know I'll have an accident," she argued.

"I know the odds!"

"Well, how about the odds where you're concerned?" she cried. "How many policemen die every year?"

"That's different!"

"How is it different?"

"I'm an adult! I can take care of myself! I've had training!"

She pounced onto that last statement like a general springing a trap on an unwary opponent. "I can get all the training you could want! They give drivers' training at school, and the county gives defensive driving courses that can lower the cost of insurance. *Plus* I have my very own personal police trainer right here. What more could you want?"

Evans could only gape at the neatness of her campaign. He shook his head to clear it as much as to redefine his objections. "B-but there's still the expense, and—"

"I'll pay for it out of my salary!" she exclaimed. "It'll have to be a used car, of course. I couldn't afford very much, but you know cars better than anyone. You could help me find a really good buy, something affordable but in decent shape."

He was still shaking his head, but inside he had to admit she was making a certain amount of sense. Still, the freedom that a car of her own would give her frightened him deeply. "You're too young!" he blurted, but again she was prepared for him.

"I'm a year older than the state of Oklahoma says you have to be to get a driver's license," she pointed out coolly, adding, "and Amy was seventeen when she got her first car. She told me so. She told me her parents—"

Evans thought his head would explode. "Amy!" he roared. "Amy Slater has nothing to do with this!"

Mattie was clearly shocked and puzzled by his outburst. She glared at him distrustfully, as if he might at any moment start foaming at the mouth. "Amy's my friend! She—"

"She has nothing to say about anything in this house!" he shouted.

"She's my friend!" Mattie shouted back.

"I'm your father!"

"That's not fair! She talks to me like an equal, an adult! She knows that if I've got sense enough to run this house, I've got sense enough to make some of my own decisions! She actually *likes* me. Just as I am, she likes me!"

Mattie dropped her head to the tabletop, her folded arms muffling her sobs as her words rang in Evans's mind. *She actually likes me! She likes me!* Merciful heaven, she couldn't actually believe that he *didn't* like her, could she? Could he have made her think that her own father didn't *like* her? He swallowed his anger and got up from his chair, moving quickly to lay his hand on her head. She was so small, so delicate, his Mattie.

"I'm sorry, sweetheart. I never meant to… You have to know that I don't just *like* you, I *love* you. You're my sunshine, my angel, my sweet baby girl. I'll always—"

Suddenly Mattie was on her feet, her emerald eyes glittering hard in the dribbling mess of her eyeliner. "You just don't get it, do you? I'm not your baby anything! That's the whole point!"

"You're my daughter!" he said sternly. "No matter how old you get, you'll always be my—"

"Oh, what's the use?" she cried, stamping her foot.

Well, if she was going to act like a baby, he was going to treat her like one! "That's quite enough, Matilda. Now go to your room until you can behave reasonably."

She threw up her hands, snorting laughter. "Go to my room, Daddy? I don't think so!" With that she whirled and banged out the back door.

He stood gaping, unable to believe what had just happened. By the time he pulled himself together and stormed out onto the porch, she was already sliding through the fence in the gate at the back of the garage. "Mattie! Matilda Kincaid, you get back here!"

"I'll come back when you've calmed down!" she called out to him.

When *he* had calmed down? Anger rushed up his throat and threatened to strangle him. He wanted to roar, to throw things, to shake that little nut until her teeth rattled and— He suddenly realized that his hands were balled into fists in front of his face. Anger vanished. Shame washed over him. When *he* calmed down. Dear God! He sat down with a thump on the edge of the porch and stared across his yard in the direction in which his daughter had disappeared. Just now, *little* Matilda had acted with far more maturity than he had. And he knew that it wasn't the notion of Mattie having her own car that had driven him over the edge it was Amy. The whole idea that Mattie was welcomed by Amy as both a friend and equal while he was not rankled him unbearably. And he'd taken it out on Mattie. No wonder she preferred Amy's company to his! He closed his eyes and began planning an apology. He was getting good at apologizing, better than he ought to be.

Chapter Six

Mattie got out of the truck glumly and literally dragged her feet as she walked toward the church. "Do we really have to do this?"

"For heaven's sake," Evans said impatiently, "it's a social, Mattie, not a hanging. You attend services without a squawk, then bellyache about going to a little party. It makes absolutely no sense to me."

"*You* won't get stuck with a bunch of immature, judgmental gossips," Mattie grumbled.

Evans sighed and stopped in the middle of the sidewalk, trying to hold on to his temper. They had only recently made peace after their last battle. He was determined not to let anger separate them again. "Honey, don't let your insecurities lead you around by the nose," he said when she stopped beside him. "You don't know that these kids talk about you. You feel conspicuous, so you assume everyone's staring and whispering behind your back, when they probably aren't doing that at all." He paused to discover what she thought about his thesis and was pleased to find her pensively silent. He decided that it was time to take a chance on praise. "By the way, I haven't told you how really lovely you look this evening. That's a very pretty dress." *About six inches too short but pretty,* he amended silently. "And your makeup looks professionally done. You could be a model." He made no mention of her hair, for though she had left off the weird neon colors, the front portion still stood almost on end.

She literally preened, fluffing the tiny, puffed sleeves and smoothing the princess seams of her little flower print dress. Evans was truly bemused by the way the pale green background and the bright blue and dark green flowers brought out the rich jewel tone of her emerald eyes. He was very pleased that she had apparently taken to heart the bit of advice he had given her about trying to fit in—but dared not say so. Nevertheless, it wouldn't kill her to give a little credit where credit was due. He cleared his throat.

"It, um, occurs to me that you've made some…adjustments in your general appearance. I was, ah, wondering why."

She shrugged and tossed a lock of long, sleek, black hair off one shoulder, then looked down at legs and feet encased in sandals with laces that crisscrossed almost to her knees. "Well…all that radical stuff, you know, the really heavy makeup and bright hair colors and monochrome clothes, that was like a mask. I was, like, hiding behind it while I tried to figure out who I really am, see?"

Evans was stunned by her acuity, so much so that he blurted out his surprise. "You actually realized this all by yourself?"

She shuffled her dainty feet. "Um, not exactly. It was… well, it was…Amy."

Amy. Hurt erupted in his chest, billowing like the mushroom of an A-bomb. "A-Amy?" he stammered.

Mattie threw out her arms. "I can talk to her, Dad! She knows where I'm coming from. She understands me, some-times better than I do myself. I'm in limbo here. I just don't have enough in common with people my own age, but I don't belong in *your* bracket, either. I'm, like, in between, you know? And it's hard, really hard. I mean, where am I going to find friends as in between as me?"

He didn't know how to answer her. He was still reeling from all she'd told him, and the thought of Amy kept echoing through his head. He needed to understand her role in this. "S-so Amy's you're only friend then? Are you saying that she's 'in between,' too?"

Mattie shook her head. "That's not it exactly. It's more like she's been where I am."

He gulped. "I—I see." Amy had more in common with his daughter than he did. She connected with Mattie—but not with him. He turned and absently started toward the church once more. He didn't see the look of compassion his daughter gave him before she hurried to catch up and fell in at his side.

They walked around the building to the park behind, a broad area of lush, lovingly tended grass interspersed with tall, mature shade trees. As they drew near the picnickers gathered on blankets spread on the ground, Evans tried to put aside his pain and disquiet, telling himself that he should be grateful that anyone could get through to Mattie, even Amy. God knew she'd given him more than one insight into his daughter. He just couldn't help wishing that it was anyone but her. Nevertheless, when Mattie slipped her arm through his, he found a smile for her. It wasn't her fault, after all, that Amy was better with her than her own father or that Amy wanted no part of him. He supposed that he should be grateful his daughter still did. The warmth seemed to have gone out of the afternoon light, though, which said nothing about the heat. It was, however, slightly cooler under the trees.

Reverend Charles spotted them and instantly moved forward, his baby daughter cradled against him with one arm, her tiny hands clutching fistfuls of his deep blue sport shirt.

"Hey, Evans, who's that beauty on your arm? Goodness gracious, is that you, Mattie?"

"I told her she looks like a model," Evans said proudly.

Mattie beamed, then held out her arms. "Can I hold the baby?"

Bolton Charles smiled doubtfully. "I'm not sure she'll let you. She's going through a clingy stage. Doesn't want me out of her sight right now."

"Oh, she just knows who adores her most," Mattie said, tickling the baby under the chin. "Don't you, baby doll?" The little one promptly loosened her hold on her father and leaned toward Mattie, both little fists latching on to strands of Mattie's long, dark hair.

Bolton gave her up laughingly. "It must be the hair. She'll hardly even go to her mother right now. Clarice thinks its because she's away at college three mornings a week, but I'm away even more often than that. I think it's this father-daughter thing, that sort of mystical connection between dads and their girls."

Evans felt that his own connection with Mattie had stretched nearly to the breaking point. He glanced at her, shocked to see that a casual observer might have mistaken her for the baby's mother. She was cooing to the little one, seemingly oblivious to the yanking of her hair. He swallowed a sudden lump in his throat and said to the minister, "Enjoy it while you can. It doesn't always last."

Bolton clapped him on the back. "It's hard to let them go, isn't it?" he said softly. "They grow up whether we want them to or not."

"Some of them grow up faster than others," Evans muttered.

Bolton nodded knowingly. "I've noticed that. She seems really good with children." He smiled compassionately at Evans's bleak look. "Come on. Let's grab a couple of cold drinks and find a basket of fried chicken." He called out to Mattie, "When you get tired of her, just take her to her mom, over there on the red blanket."

"Oh, I won't get tired of her," Mattie replied, gathering her hair into one hand and pulling it aside. She jiggled the baby. "We'll just play and play, won't we, angel?" The baby patted Mattie's cheeks and put her nose to Mattie's, babbling and drooling at the same time.

Bolton chuckled. "I think I've been dethroned. Well, maybe we've acquired another baby-sitter in the trade."

"Oh, could I?" Mattie said eagerly. "I've been looking for a part-time job, and I love kids!"

"Consider yourself hired. I'll speak to Clarice, and one of us will call you."

Mattie put her head back, hugged the baby tight, and spun around in celebration. The baby giggled with innocent joy.

Evans followed Bolton toward a large ice chest sitting beneath a tree. It was comforting to see Mattie so happy— and disturbing to think of her as being *employed*. Bolton seemed to sense his conflicting emotions.

"Maybe I spoke too quickly," the minister said. "Perhaps you don't want Mattie baby-sitting."

Evans shook his head. "It's not that really. It's just..." He shook his head again, at a momentary loss for words. "She's, um, been talking about getting her own car, and I'm just not ready for that yet."

Bolton bent and reached into the ice chest, coming up with a cola, which he handed to Evans before going back for another. "I think I know how you feel. Letting go really is hard to do."

Evans popped the top on his drink. "You don't seem to have much trouble with it."

Bolton straightened, laughing. "You should've felt the bottom drop out of my stomach when my kid practically threw herself out of my arms and into Mattie's."

Evans sipped his drink, smiling. "Yeah, I remember that feeling well. Seems like it was only yesterday that it happened to me."

Bolton sighed. "That's the way of it all right. I suspect those memories, the immediacy and intensity of them, are God's way of sharpening our joy—and also of teaching us how impermanent this life is."

"You can say that again," Evans agreed. "It not only changes, it changes *fast*. Trust me."

Bolton slugged back about half his drink, sighed with pleasure and smiled at Evans. "I think you're a man whose friendship I should definitely cultivate. You can terrify me about all the traumas I have ahead of me."

Evans laughed, relaxing. "If I were you, I'd run like the dickens in the opposite direction, bury my head in the sand and live in blissful ignorance as long as possible."

Bolton lifted his drink in a mock salute. "Sounds like the voice of experience to me."

They butted cans, then turned and wandered beneath the trees. Neither man doubted he'd made a friend.

It was some time later that Bolton introduced Evans to Griff Shaw. "Another member of the brotherhood," he said. "Men with daughters who wrap them around pretty little pinkies without even trying."

Griff laughed. "Oh, man, ain't it the truth. We don't stand a chance. That gal of mine has led me around by a ring in my nose right from the very beginning. Worst part is, I love it."

Evans liked him already. He was definitely all cowboy, from the crown of his hat to the soles of his boots. He was also open and friendly and outgoing, inviting Evans to sit on his blanket and share his barbecue when Bolton spotted another new arrival that needed a welcome. "My wife's off visiting somewhere, but she'll be around soon. Where's your lady?"

Evans smiled gently. "My wife's deceased."

Griff swept off his hat. "Oh, I am sorry."

"Thanks, but it's been a long time now."

"Never remarried, huh?"

Evans shrugged. "Never found another right woman."

"Yeah, it takes the right one, all right," Griff agreed. "Now you take me. I didn't think I'd ever get married—even after I found the right one! My reputation kind of preceded me, and I had to battle it before I could convince her. Actually, what saved it for me, I think, was Danna. That's our little girl. She adopted me as her daddy before I even knew that's what I wanted to be. Man, she is something! Bright as a new penny, sweet as candy, pretty as a picture. Got practically the whole rodeo circuit eating out of her hand!"

Evans laughed loud and long. Now here was a smitten father! "No wonder she got her aunt Amy to promise to quit smoking!"

Griff's smile abruptly waned. "You know my sister-in-law?"

Evans nodded. "We live next door to her."

"Oh, your daughter must be Mattie!"

"That's right. I take it Amy's mentioned her."

"And how," Griff said, plopping his hat in his lap and leaning back on his arms. "She's real taken with that kid, though I guess she's not a kid in the same sense as mine. Amy says she's seventeen going on thirty."

Evans groaned and dropped his forehead to one drawn up knee. "I guess I let Mattie grow up too fast after her mother died, and now I'm regretting it. I'm not ready for my little girl to be a young woman!"

Griff grinned and fitted his hat onto his head again. "I don't think you have to worry too much about Mattie. She seems real smart from what Amy says. My wife thinks she's a godsend. Heaven knows she's brought real change to Amy's life." His eyes narrowed suddenly. "Or somebody has."

Evans shook his head. "Don't look at me. Amy can't stand me. She and Mattie are thick as thieves, though. Mattie did help her clean up her house and get it organized. She's real good at that kind of thing. Speaking of good influences, though, I'd say your daughter started it by getting Amy to quit smoking."

Griff shrugged. "It's hard to deny Danna anything, she's such a sweetie. But Danna and Joan have been after Amy to stop smoking for a long time. I think Amy just finally started pulling up out of that depression she's been living in."

"Depression?" Evans echoed.

Griff stretched out his legs and crossed them at the ankles. "Jo says it started even before her husband got sick. She didn't think much of the fellow, said he was selfish and controlling. Apparently he was some older than Amy. He married her young—over her parents' objections, I take it—and made her into just what he wanted her to be. Jo thinks Amy was unhappy almost from the first but couldn't or wouldn't admit it. She says Amy convinced herself they had this great love and held on to the notion all the tighter as things got worse. Since he died, Amy's wallowed around in this dark pit of grief and guilt, and now that she's starting to climb out of it, she's afraid. Anyway, that's the way Jo sees it. She even thinks Amy would've been better off if he hadn't left her fixed well enough to get by without a job. Having to support herself would have at least gotten her out of the house."

Evans lifted a brow thoughtfully. It made a certain sense. In fact, it matched well with what he'd observed of Amy himself. *And it gives you an excuse to go back for more,* he admitted silently. *Maybe it wasn't you at all. Maybe it was the fear.*

He tamped down the flare of hope that he felt, telling himself that it didn't really make much difference *why* Amy didn't want him around, only that she didn't. Or did she? He doubted she knew what she wanted, which, he realized with a flash of insight, was one more thing she had in common with Mattie! She had certainly reached out in that direction. Maybe what Amy needed was the same thing that Mattie seemed to need, a friend of her own age and experience, someone who at least knew what she'd gone through in losing a spouse. He couldn't seem to befriend his own daughter—and maybe that was the way it was supposed to be—but he could at least try to befriend Amy. He might even be able to reestablish certain ties with his daughter through Amy as a mutual friend.

And maybe later friendship would blossom into something more. Maybe Amy would find that she shared this attraction he felt. But that could come later. Right now, he'd serve them all better by being a good neighbor and friend.

Oddly enough, Evans felt as if some of the cloud over his head had lifted. When he caught sight of Mattie sitting on the grass surrounded by half a dozen entranced children, he smiled and pointed her out to Griffin Shaw with pride. Griff returned the favor by pointing out that one of those entranced kids was his own little daughter, who was everything he'd said she was, her copper-bright hair glistening around a perfect little face lit by a secure, happy smile.

When Griff's wife, Joan, returned from her round of visits, Evans got to his feet and met her with genuine eagerness. She had the same bright hair as her daughter, but the eyes, the nose, and the chin were all Amy. Even the build was similar.

Joan was a no-nonsense sort with a heart like melted butter and an inner strength that Evans somehow recognized as akin to his own. He was prepared to like her at once but understood that her own judgment concerning him would be delayed until she was satisfied that he was all he seemed. As a man who made no apologies about who and what he was, Evans had no qualms about that. He wished Amy could be so open-minded. It didn't take long for him to realize that Joan had already met Mattie, about whom Amy had apparently spoken very highly.

"Amy's right," she said flatly, after being introduced to Evans and having Mattie pointed out. "She's a natural. In fact," she went on, dropping down onto the blanket next to her husband, whose arms immediately slipped around her, "I'd say Amy doesn't know the half of it. From here, Mattie looks like a natural mother as well as a homemaker."

"Whoa!" Evans laughed. "Let's don't rush her. She's still a kid herself."

Joan exchanged a look with her clearly adoring husband before smiling almost secretively. That smile unsettled Evans, as it seemed to indicate that he wasn't being realistic, but he knew his own daughter, didn't he? Who could know Mattie better than he did? He was busy convincing himself that Mattie was indeed the child he believed her to be, only vaguely aware that the Shaws were carrying on a conversation around him, until Joan leaned forward and laid a small, pale hand upon his forearm. His attention and gaze snapped around to her face.

"We really do owe you a debt of thanks," she was saying, "and I don't mean just for the yard work and other things."

He could only blink at her. "Oh, that. That's nothing, just neighborly concern."

"Call it whatever you like," Joan said meaningfully, "but I can't help thinking you've had something to do with Amy finally beginning to come out of her shell."

He shook his head at that. "If that's really happening, it's more a matter of timing than anything else. Believe me, your sister harbors no affection for me. Mattie's the one with the influence."

"Maybe so," Joan said, unconvinced. Her eyes were teasing, sparkling. "You certainly do seem to rub her the wrong way."

Evans grimaced at both the meaning and the implication

of that remark. "Amy's just so darn prickly," he complained, and Joan laughed outright.

"My point exactly." Before he could challenge that, she launched into a long discourse about the church and its many services and programs, ending as Bolton Charles returned by saying that they all hoped Evans and Mattie would soon join them formally.

Bolton seconded that. "In fact, I was wondering if you'd let me call on you next week to discuss that very matter."

Evans agreed readily, and they set the visit for an afternoon later in the week. Afterward, Bolton decreed it time to get the eating done and move on to the games. Evans stood watching the activity and a sense of peace stole over him, a sense of rightness and belonging, of home. He mentally released the hurt and worries and aggravations that had bedeviled him, and for the first time since he'd come to Duncan, he really felt that he was exactly where he should be, that all would be well. Eventually.

Amy stared a long time at her reflection in the mirror. *Well, you almost blew it, girl,* she told herself sardonically, *over a little thing like a kiss.* Her conscience kicked her smartly, and she shook her head. All right, it wasn't a little thing, that kiss. It had been a swift plunge into reality, followed by a desperate flight into denial facilitated by destructive old habits. *Well, not too destructive,* she mused, eyeing her reflection critically.

She had lost a little weight, but of course she needed to lose more and to tone up her muscles. Her skin was clean and unblemished, if almost pasty pale, and her hair was both shinier and longer than it had been in quite some time. She wondered if she ought to cut it and decided that it didn't matter really. The weight was the important thing just now. She took a deep breath, tightening her resolve, and noticed how her eyes seemed a touch brighter than usual, or was it simply that her mood had finally lifted after a veritable orgy of recrimination, self-pity and regret.

She turned away from her dresser mirror and wandered over to the bed, but she wasn't really tired. God knew she'd spent enough time with her head beneath the covers of late. She wasn't absolutely clear that she had come to any real understanding with herself. Perhaps her marriage had not been the idyll she had wanted to believe, but her grief and despair at Mark's death was as real as anything could be, and she still could not quite reconcile his death with the world as she knew it. Maybe it was the way he had died, the long, lingering, debilitating illness that had taken him from a strong, vibrant, even overpowering man to a fragile, pathetic and, yes, petty weakling.

She still couldn't understand how God could allow such a thing to happen, especially as she had prayed and begged and tried so hard to believe in His mercy. Mark himself had told her that she was not being realistic, but she couldn't help feeling that it was her own fear that had defeated them both in the end. Did God punish us for our fears? In nearly three years now, she had not figured out an answer to that question. Perhaps it was time to look elsewhere, to Reverend Charles, perhaps? She felt instinctively that he would be willing, even glad, to discuss the matter, but she didn't think that she could quite bring herself to ask it of him. She could ask Evans—if he was speaking to her.

She wouldn't blame him if he wasn't. She had reacted with bald foolishness to his kiss, and she could admit to herself now that she regretted doing so. Even as she made the admission, however, she whispered a plea for forgiveness, not to God, but to Mark, then she threw herself on the bed in fresh misery. She was tired of being married to a dead man, tired of imagining his disappointment in her, tired of feeling disloyal simply for living. She just wasn't quite certain how to break the cycle. Quite deliberately, she directed her thoughts back to their former track. Perhaps she couldn't break free of the emotional bondage in which Mark or God or both had placed her, but she could do something about her appearance.

She hadn't slept well and had used that as an excuse for lounging around most of the day, but what she really needed was not rest but exercise, and by golly she was going to get it. Buoyed by determination, she sprang up and threw off her bed clothes, jerking on in their place a soft bra, a roomy T-shirt, a pair of knit shorts, thick socks and her athletic shoes. She whisked a brush through her hair, then grabbed an elasticized headband from a drawer and slipped it on, tucking it behind her ears in order to keep her hair off her face. That done, she swept out of the house and across the yard, turning on the sidewalk to move swiftly down the street toward the intersection.

The day was hot but her determination was hotter. She lifted her chin and swung her arms at her sides, setting her destination as the park that fronted 81 near Beech and the Halliburton Football Stadium. She was sweaty and out of breath by the time she stepped into the shade beneath the sheltering arms of the welcome old trees in the park, but experience told her that if she sat down now, fatigue would overtake her and she'd lose the determination that had driven her thus far. She allowed herself a few quick gulps of water from a public drinking fountain then fell into stride once more, walking back and forth beneath the trees for some minutes before turning for home.

She was trembling by the time she turned down her street but proud of herself for sticking with it. If her skin felt clammy and red-hot at the same time, she supposed it had to do with the perspiration pouring from her and a light sunburn. Next time, she told herself as she blindly put one foot in front of another, she'd remember to use a sunscreen and bring along a water bottle. She was dragging herself across her yard when she stumbled and went down, sitting hard on her bottom as the world tilted and spun.

"Good grief!"

She didn't recognize the voice as Evans's, but when her vision cleared, it was focused upon him as he hurried away from his drive toward her. She saw the lawn mower turned on its side and the running water hose beside it with which he'd been cleaning the blades. She looked down at her hands planted in the grass and realized cheerfully that he'd mowed her lawn again. She smiled up at him as he drew near, noting as she did so that her neck felt weak and rubbery.

"Are you trying to kill yourself?" he demanded, yanking her up and wrapping his arm around her waist.

"I went for a walk," she said inanely as he half dragged, half carried her back the way he'd come.

"So I noticed," he growled, letting her down on the little slope that fell away to his drive. "Didn't it occur to you not to start this sort of thing in the heat of the day?"

She lay back on the grass, panting weakly. "Guess I'm more out of condition than I thought."

"You've nearly given yourself a heat stroke, you little idiot. Lie still and let me cool you off." He was back with the hose in two seconds, splashing the cool water over her legs. She bolted upright when he raised the hose to her hips. "Don't," he ordered sternly, letting the water run over her shoulders, chest and back before lifting it to her head. "You'll dry off soon enough in this heat. Now sit there and drink." He thrust the hose into her hands and watched, hands on hips, while she gulped down the rubbery tasting water. "That's enough," he said, grabbing back the hose and letting the water pour over her head again.

Her sanity restored, she pushed his hands away and slumped over her knees. "Thanks. Guess I overdid it."

He doubled the hose and gripped it to shut off the water, then picked a dry spot and sat down beside her. "There's nothing wrong with getting some exercise," he told her mildly, "but there are better times for it."

"Yeah?" She pushed the sodden headband off the back of her head and squeezed the water out of it. "When would you suggest?"

He shrugged. "Early morning is the best time, I guess. For years I hit the pavement every morning before daylight. My work schedule makes that impossible now, of course, but I know I'd feel better if I could work it in."

"Maybe you could try a quick run in the morning after you get off work," she proposed helpfully.

"Didn't Mattie tell you?" he asked, smiling. "I've made it all the way up to the second rung of the ladder. I'll be leading a seminormal life from now on, reporting early in the afternoon, getting off around midnight."

"Oh, that's great!"

He nodded, seeming pleased. "I'll miss seeing Mattie when she comes home from school, but I'll still be up with her in the mornings, and I've arranged to take a long dinner break every evening, so I can be home then."

"That's wonderful," Amy said, somewhat surprised at the easiness she felt with him, the genuine friendliness of his smile and tone. "Maybe you could have that run at night after you get off work. It'll be cool then and there won't be much traffic."

He nodded. "I don't see why not."

"I favor the night myself," she rambled on, squinting up into the sunlight. "I've never been much of a morning person."

He chuckled. "So I've noticed. Tell me, what route did you take?"

"Oh, I went down to the park. You know, the one off the bypass. The football field's near there, too. I suppose you could use the track there if you wanted to, and then there's the Simmon's Center, but I don't know if it would be open at that time of night."

"I prefer to run out of doors," he said decisively. "The park ought to do nicely. I'll drive by that way later and check the distance on my odometer."

She looked up sheepishly. "Oh, I didn't think of that. It was a spur-of-the-moment decision for me. I just wanted to *do* something, you know?"

He nodded and got to his feet, offering her his free hand. "Very commendable, just do it at the right time from now on."

"All right." She smiled at him and put her hand in his, allowing him to pull her to her feet. She grimaced as stiffening muscles protested.

"You'd better have a good stretch before you shower and change," he told her. "Do you know what to do?"

"I think so."

"Good. Well, I'll let you get to it."

He started back down to the mower, while she turned and forced her sore legs up the little slope. There she stopped and turned back, calling out his name. He turned and looked up at her. "You didn't have to mow the yard," she said, "but thank you."

His smile was quick and broad. "My pleasure."

"I—I want to say that I'm sorry, too," she said stumbling on, "for...the last time."

His smile faded, but no hint of anger or censure dimmed the softness of his gaze. "It was more my fault than yours. I shouldn't have—"

"No!" she interrupted firmly. "I overreacted, much more so than you even know, but in the end...well, let's just say that it worked out for the best and leave it at that."

He looked down at the dribbling water hose in his hand, then up again, and she could tell by the look on his face that the matter had been put away, never to be taken out again. "You have that stretch now," he told her, loosening the hose, but then his voice dropped low and silky as he said, "I wouldn't want to see you in pain."

She smiled as he turned to target the hose once more on the mower blade. It was worth a little pain, she told herself as she moved stiffly toward her house, to see and hear his concern again. It was, in fact, worth a good deal more.

Chapter Seven

Amy stretched yet again, relieved that her muscles merely complained this time instead of screaming. She had been so stiff and sore when she'd gotten out of bed that morning that she could hardly move. She had immediately begun to worry. She couldn't be *that* out of shape. A call to her doctor and a frank discussion had put her fears to rest, however, as it was his opinion that her extreme soreness was as much a product of heat exhaustion as exercise. He advised her to keep comfortably warm, not cool, to drink plenty of fluids, to stretch, stretch and stretch again, and to take herself out for a short walk in the cool of the evening. Afterward, she was to stretch again every time she felt her muscles stiffening up. She was mildly surprised that he advised her to continue her exercise program, stretching before and after and working out in the coolest part of the day. Proper conditioning, he told her, was the healthiest solution.

She did exactly what he told her, taking her walk about ten in the evening. She kept it short indeed, traveling only to the end of the street and back, but just that much exercise loosened her up amazingly. Since then, she'd stretched about every half hour, and now—just after midnight—she was feeling pleasantly energized and…bored.

The sound of a vehicle passing caught her attention. She got up off the floor and went to the window. Evans's pickup was turning into his drive. Amy bit her lip, seized by a sudden desire to run out and go to him. If she left now, she could catch him between the garage and the house. And say what? Do what? She sank down on a chair next to the window and hung over the arm, staring out the window for a glimpse of him. He was probably tired, she told herself. He'd want to see Mattie before she went to sleep. Amy knew for a fact that Mattie had intended to wait up for him. She ought to just go to bed herself and forget about him. But she didn't. Instead, she sat there staring out of the window hungrily, noting as lights went on and off in Evans's house, as he moved through it. Then finally all the visible lights went off, and she sat back, her watch desultory now.

She wasn't even particularly watching for him anymore when she caught a flicker of movement out of the corner of her eye and pitched forward again over the arm of the chair. She caught sight of Evans coming up the gentle slope of her yard, the white of his sleeveless T-shirt shining almost as brightly as the orange fluorescent stripe angling across it. She realized suddenly that he was dressed for running and jumped up in excitement. She was still dressed in the clothes she had worn for her walk earlier. She could just step out on her porch as he passed and pretend that she was about to go out for some exercise, too.

But then he'd be almost obligated to ask her to come along with him, and when she couldn't keep up, he'd be put out with her and that would be the end of that. He'd start walking around the other way in order to avoid her, and she'd never see him again.

Sighing, she sat back down in the chair, only to jump up again as footsteps sounded clearly on her own porch. She yanked the door open even as he knocked. He nearly fell into the room. Laughing, he righted himself and leaned against the doorframe, arms folded, legs crossed at the ankles. "At least you're ready," he said.

She lifted her eyebrows. "Ready?"

"For our run."

Her mouth fell open. "Our…? Oh. Well, sure. Of course. Wh-what'd you think?"

He shrugged. "Well, it occurred to me that you might be too sore to go out tonight, but you seem to have fared better than I expected."

She grinned. "Actually, I've been stretching all day. I, um, even took a short walk earlier."

"Great! I was afraid that when we set this up yesterday we might have been too optimistic."

Set this up yesterday, had they? She thought back over their conversation and smiled to herself. Yes, she could see how he might have assumed that they were going out on this run together. He might have actually asked, though. On the other hand, she wasn't about to point that out to him now. "Ready when you are," she said brightly.

He nodded and headed through the door. She followed on his heels, pulling the door closed behind her. "Come on," he said, dropping into a slow exercise, "one more stretch won't hurt you, and I want to be sure that you're doing it properly."

Amy nodded and followed his example as closely as she was able.

"Good," he said, watching her slow, steady movements before switching to another position.

She followed suit, keeping her motions slow and careful from necessity. Soon Evans was satisfied with her preparation, and they walked down the steps and across the yard, turning onto the sidewalk. They picked up the pace a bit, Evans explaining that he'd have to ease into a jog gradually since he hadn't been working out regularly for several weeks. That suited Amy, who hadn't worked out regularly at all, just fine.

All too soon, though, she found herself trotting alongside him and then struggling to keep up as he picked up the pace yet again. By the time they reached the park, her lungs were screaming for oxygen and her legs were threatening to fold with every step. She was determined to hold out, but something of her distress must have communicated itself, for as soon as they reached the trees, Evans drew up, shook out his long limbs and began walking her around the picnic tables, his arm locked firmly about her waist.

"Boy, I'm really out of shape," he lied, barely having broken a sweat. Amy smiled weakly at his attempt to spare her and let him move her around and around beneath the trees, trusting him to find their way through the deep shadows. Finally, he gently pushed her onto a concrete bench and climbed up onto the table at her back to dangle his long legs over the side near her shoulder.

Traffic moved lightly up and down the 81 Bypass on the

far side of the playground, its noise a mere hum. Night sounds surpassed it, the gentle clicking of crickets and the occasional whir of a june bug seeking light, the sigh of a breeze wading through the treetops far overhead. It was oddly peaceful there in the shadows, life whispering around them.

"This is nice," Evans said softly. "Andie and I used to walk out on evenings like this before Mattie was born. We couldn't really afford movies or restaurant dinners back then, so we'd just stroll out at night for something to do." He leaned forward, bracing his hands on the edge of the table. "Our apartment was about a mile from the beach. We'd walk down there at night and sit in this little cove behind a really tall sand dune. It was private property, I think, but nobody ever said anything to us. I doubt they even knew we were there. We'd just sit on the sand and watch the water and talk about things. Sometimes we'd stop off and buy a beer on the way, or just a cola." He paused for a time, and she could hear him smile. "We'd have been happy with a paper cup of water," he said. "I imagine you and your husband had times like that."

Amy thought a moment, then shook her head. "Not really. Mark wasn't the sort to take pleasure in simple things. He had very definite goals in life, and he went about achieving them thoughtfully and methodically."

"Such as?" Evans prodded.

She cocked her head, remembering. "Well, for one thing, he had very firm ideas about marriage and finances. Finances definitely came first. He even had a dollar amount that he wanted in the bank before he would marry. Once he had it, he went wife hunting."

"And found you," Evans surmised.

"And found me," she confirmed. "A promotion was part of

the plan, too, and as soon as he got it, we set a date. My parents thought it was all rather cold-blooded, but I admired his drive."

"And so you married him."

"Umm-hmm. We had a very lovely wedding, very formal and traditional. He wanted it that way. He was a very involved bridegroom."

"I'll bet he was," Evans said mildly, adding, "I couldn't have cared less how we did it, so long as she married me."

"Mark wanted everything perfect," she said rather defensively.

He chuckled. "So did Andie, and what made Andie happy made me happy."

She turned her head to look at him in amazement, for that was exactly how she'd felt about Mark. "I know what you mean. I really do."

He dropped a large, hot hand onto the top of her head, then slid it down to her nape and left it there. "Love really opens us up, doesn't it? We do things for love that we'd never think of doing otherwise."

"Yeah," Amy said on a sigh, leaning her head back against the stone table and allowing Evans's hand to cushion it. "No matter what it takes to please that person in the center of your universe, you do it."

Evans was quiet a moment, then he said, "Andie was easy to please. She had all these romantic ideas, and it was really fun to make them happen. She appreciated the smallest things, candles on the dinner table, roses picked off the neighbor's bush. I got this silly little ring out of a vending machine once, and I took it home and made a big deal out of giving it to her. We said our wedding vows again in front of an open window, so all the world could see. I lived to give her those little moments."

Amy stared up into the swaying treetops dreamily, spotting a single star here and another there. "I know just what you mean," she said, "not that Mark was particularly easy to please. He wasn't, really. He had extremely high standards, but he was wonderfully, wildly appreciative when I reached them."

"That's great," Evans said neutrally, "so long as you live up to expectations."

Amy nodded. Maybe she hadn't lived up to Mark's expectations quite as often as he would have liked, but the times that she had, had been wonderful, and she was determined to hold on to that. The other times, she would just keep to herself. Some tiny part of her, though, wondered what it would have been like to have lived in the radiance of his love all the time, as Evans intimated he had done with his Andie. But then, no one was deliriously happy all the time. Were they? She hesitantly put that question to Evans, who agreed with her.

"It's the little things that drive you crazy sometimes, isn't it?" he said. "For me it was chomping ice. Andie loved to chomp ice. I'd have to leave the room or something to keep from shouting at her. Then she'd realize what she was doing, stop it, and come and get me. Or sometimes she'd just chomp even louder and laugh at me. Either way, she never gave it up, and I never stopped hating it."

Amy sat up straight again, thinking. "Mark wouldn't have put up with that," she told him. "He'd have said that if I loved him, a little thing like that ought to have been easy to give up."

"Yeah, but by the same token," Evans argued lightly, "a little thing like that ought to be easy to put up with if you love somebody."

Amy frowned. "I guess you and Andie were just more easygoing than Mark and I. His...*our* tolerance for such things was considerably lower."

"Hey, don't get me wrong," Evans said quickly. "Andie was easy to please, but she had a temper, believe me, and when she got mad, boy-oh-boy!" He shook his head, grinning. "I remember once we had a hostage situation downtown. It was real touch-and-go stuff. Everybody was right on the edge, you know, real intense. So that when it all worked out okay and we got everybody out safe with only one of our guys wounded, there was this kind of jubilant mood that swept through the whole force. Anyway, I guess I got caught up in it all, and I didn't stop to think that Andie would have heard about it on the news and be worried for me. So I walk blithely into the house after hoisting a few with the boys in celebration, and Andie pops me square on the chin." He chuckled. "She wasn't big enough to hurt me, but man, was she up for it that night! Thinking back on it, I'm surprised she didn't knock my block off with a baseball bat or something."

"Thinking about it now," Amy rejoined dryly, "I don't think I'd blame her."

"Hey, I learned my lesson the first time," Evans said. "After that if some bozo so much as backed into a police cruiser, I called in to let her know it wasn't mine. I think it made a difference, too. Police work in a big city is hard on marriages. I can't tell you how many of our friends' marriages busted up over the years, or how many of them dropped out or went to booze...or worse."

"But you two hung in there," she said softly. "I'm impressed, Evans. How did you do it?"

"We worked at it," he told her. "We worked *hard* at it. We did everything we could think of to strengthen the bond."

"And then some drunk in a van took her out," Amy whispered. "Sometimes don't you wonder if God's paying any attention?"

Evans pushed a hand through his hair, clearly trying to decide how to answer that. "You could look at it that way, I guess," he finally said, "but I can't help thinking what my life would have been like if she hadn't been part of it. How can I blame God for taking her away from me and not acknowledge Him for bringing her to me in the first place?"

Amy bit her lip. "I see what you mean."

"Andie taught me things nobody else could have," Evans said. "She touched me in a way I didn't even know I could be touched. She showed me a quality of life I'd never have known existed otherwise. I don't—can't—believe that was all an accident. And I know that if God had intended my life to end when hers did, He'd have taken me out, too." He sighed and shook his head. "I don't pretend to know *why* it all happened, but I cannot believe that it was all for nothing. I won't believe that."

Amy took a deep breath and silently let it out again. "I never thought of it that way," she said meekly. "I wish I had. Maybe I wouldn't have felt as though I had nothing to live for after Mark died."

Evans slid his arm across her shoulders. "Amy," he said, his tone mixed, equal parts censure and compassion. "I know I had Mattie to hold on to, but you have people, too, people who love you and need you. You have your family."

She felt tears well in her eyes. Family. She'd closed them

out with everyone else, partly because they hadn't liked Mark and partly because she couldn't bring herself to admit that Mark might have earned their dislike. He hadn't wanted anyone else to make demands on her time or loyalty or regard—and she hadn't been able to face the fact that it was as much from selfishness as for love of her. *Oh, Mark,* she thought, *I let you down. I was selfish, too. I should have faced our problems head-on and made us both be better than we were, instead of pretending that I was adored beyond all reason. You were right. I couldn't face reality then, but I have to now or be buried alive with your memory—and my own illusions.*

"Speaking of family," Evans was saying, "I met your sister and brother-in-law the other day."

"Oh, really?"

"Umm-hmm." He got to his feet and stepped down off the bench, turning to reach out a hand to her. "We had dinner together at the church picnic," he said. "They're a neat couple. I really admire them."

"Was Danna there?" Amy asked, allowing him to haul her up to her feet on muscles gone stiff yet again.

"Yep." He lifted one foot to the bench and started stretching again. She followed suit. "I didn't really spend much time with her, though. Mattie sort of monopolized her—and all the other kids there!"

"Well, I'm not surprised," Amy commented off-handedly, concentrating on loosening up her hamstrings. "A love of kids dovetails neatly with everything else I've learned about that daughter of yours."

"Oh? How so?"

She shrugged and fell in step beside him as he began a

measured walk toward the street. "Well, Mattie's definitely the domestic sort. I mean, I don't know any other eighteen-year-olds who have Mattie's fascination with keeping house and cooking and making a home. I think she's definitely headed for the Wife-and-Mother-of-the-Year finals."

"Oh, you never can tell," Evans said tightly, swinging his arms, "she might surprise you. I've been thinking that Mattie's particular skills could translate into some very useful occupations, like nursing, for instance."

"True," Amy said, "but Mattie hasn't expressed any particular interest in nursing to me. All she's talked about to me is getting married and having a family."

"Mattie's young," Evans snapped. "Seventeen, not eighteen."

Amy disciplined a smile. "For about another month."

"Seventeen or eighteen," Evans growled, "she's too young to know what she wants out of life just yet. I think she should go to nursing school after she graduates. Then, if she meets the right guy, I won't stand in her way."

Amy stopped in her tracks and made him turn around to gape at her. "Evans Kincaid, of all the absurd notions. You can't dictate Mattie's life to her any more than your father could have dictated to you."

"I'm not trying to dictate to her! I just want her to be prepared for whatever life hands her."

"Evans, you have to know that Mattie *doesn't* want to go to college. She's tired of school. She's looking forward to graduating from high school so she won't have to go anymore!"

"You can't do anything these days without a college education!" Evans scoffed. "Of course she'll go to college!"

Amy shook her head pityingly. "Brother, for a smart guy, you sure are stupid about your own daughter."

"Don't tell me about my daughter!" he shouted. "I know my own daughter!"

"Why can't you see that she's different from other kids her age?"

"She shouldn't be different!" Evans insisted, throwing up his hands. "She'll only be a kid once! She ought to be concentrating on kid things, like school and football games and…" He stirred his hand in helpless agitation.

Amy took one of those hands in her own. "Oh, Evans," she said, "can't you see how little Mattie has in common with other kids her age? I suspect her mother was the very same way. You told me that you married her young."

"Don't be silly," he snorted. "Andie was a lot more mature than Mattie, for one thing."

"Oh, really? How so?"

He snatched his hand away, turned and started rapidly down the street. Amy once more fell in beside him, wondering if he was going to give her an answer. He did, eventually. "Andie never *ever* stiffened her hair with spray paint or ringed her eyes with black gunk," he insisted flatly.

Amy chuckled. "Just because the fashions of rebellion seemed less outrageous to you back then, Evans, doesn't mean that she didn't wear them. Believe me, when she did, her parents thought they were every bit as outrageous as Mattie's hair spray and eyeliner."

He made a face, complaining, "You don't understand!"

"Or you don't," Amy said softly beside him.

Evans hardened his jaw and picked up the pace. Amy took a deep breath and went after him. Now who refused to face reality? she asked herself, chortling. Far from being disappointed in him, she felt a sort of kinship—and the urge to be there for him when he finally opened his stubborn eyes. As he was here for her now, now that she could finally look at the past and herself with honesty and perspective. He was right, she realized humbly. These things didn't happen for no reason.

Maybe God was paying attention, after all.

Evans moved in place, shaking his hands and, on occasion, his feet, in an attempt to cool down. It was a rare morning, utterly sparkling in its brightness. He could almost feel a touch of autumn in the air, but September was barely middle-aged, and the afternoons still blazed. True autumn was still a couple of weeks away, and Evans found that he was not looking forward to it. Autumn would undoubtedly mean chilly nights, and as pleasant as it was to be out on so glorious a morning, he did not want to think of giving up his late-night runs with Amy. He liked having that dark, shadowy park all to themselves, even though it was becoming more and more difficult to play the friend when what he wanted more and more was to be the lover.

He sneaked a peak at his running partner. She had made an amazing transformation in the past few weeks. She had taken to running like a duck to water, and her diligence had paid off handsomely. He suspected that she had been working much harder than he'd realized, that she had taken herself out alone in the mornings as well as accompanying him in the evenings. Either that or she was doing something equally strenuous in the daytime, for her hair had not acquired those subtle, shining, golden highlights at the hairdresser's and her body had not melted into that svelte, willowy shape because of their nightly runs alone.

But it was more than appearance. Something inside her had changed. It was as if a door had cracked open inside her and a crystal light was beginning to shine through. Amy Slater was quickly becoming a woman any man would want, *any* man. She might not realize it yet, but Amy Slater could have her pick—and she was apt to pick any man but him, he was beginning to fear.

Certainly she had not indicated in any way, not by the slightest nuance, that she found him personally attractive or anything but a running buddy, a friend and a neighbor. She was close to Mattie, though, and Mattie had developed a great admiration and respect for her. He was frankly surprised by how much Amy was able to accomplish with Mattie, surprised and a little envious. He was Mattie's father, after all. Ought not he be the one to move his daughter onto the correct pathways? Yet, all he and Mattie seemed to do anymore was argue. She was only months away from high school graduation, after all, and her whole future was at stake. Didn't anyone but him understand that?

"Oh, it's a wonderful day, isn't it?" Amy exulted, throwing her arms out and spinning in a circle on the lawn.

Evans shook off his reverie and smiled, nodding. "Beautiful."

"I've never been much of a morning person, you know," she said, strolling toward the porch steps, "but I don't seem to require as much sleep now as I used to. One of the benefits of all this exercise, I guess." She smiled engagingly, and Evans smiled back.

"You do seem to have a lot more energy," he said, "and you're certainly looking good."

She literally twinkled. "Am I?"

"Yes."

"Well, that's nice."

Suddenly everything felt awkward. Evans moved backward, as if he had overstepped and must remove himself to a safe distance. It was a feeling he hated, and he hated it all the more for its newness, but he didn't make an excuse and turn, as he was inclined to do, and walk home. Instead, he stood, caught by the need to be with her, to have her want him as he wanted her. Dear God, he was falling in love with her. She was more to him now than an attractive woman who might one day come to fill a physical void in his life, and he wasn't at all certain that he could be happy with the idea. Loving involved risk, more risk than he had ever realized, and he had already lost more than he had ever thought he could bear. He realized suddenly that she must be struggling with that same vulnerability, and his admiration of her grew.

He opened his mouth to make his excuses after all, when she surprised him by speaking first. "Want a glass of tea? No sugar, I promise."

He chuckled, remembering that first glass of her tea that he'd tried to drink. He nodded and moved toward her. "I'd love a glass of tea, thank you."

She danced in front of him into the house, the door opening with just a turn of the knob. He was going to have to speak to her again about leaving her house unlocked. It wasn't wise, even in Duncan, for a single woman to leave her doors open while she was gone, especially for an attractive single woman. He followed her inside.

The house was clean and neat and smelled faintly of pine. The little table in the kitchen was covered with a pretty cloth and decorated with a pair of ruffled place mats and a small bouquet of flowers in a clear vase, the kind of flowers for sale at the grocery store. She was taking pains with her environment even though no one was there to see but her. Or was there? He remembered Mattie saying only the morning before that Amy had had company. He had wondered aloud if her sister had come to visit, but Mattie had said firmly that it wasn't her sister. He had bitten his tongue to keep from asking if Amy's visitor had been a man, and he had told himself half a dozen times since that it didn't matter. The important thing was that she was well and truly coming out of her shell of grief. She was beginning to live again, and she needed friends, even male friends. It didn't have to be more than that. He was her friend, after all, only her friend.

He took the glass of iced tea that she brought him and smiled his thanks before lifting it to taste it. It was surprisingly good, freshly brewed, clear and clean tasting. "Very good," he said, saluting her with the glass.

She laughed. "Mattie's been teaching me the fine art of brewing. I think I drank it so sweet before because I made such a bitter glass." She made a face, adding off-handedly, "Mark didn't drink tea, and it never occurred to me to make it good for myself." She shook her head, smiling almost secretively.

Evans wanted to pull her onto his lap and kiss her silly. Instead he leaned forward, his forearms against the tabletop. "You've certainly come a long way in a short time," he told her softly, aware that his voice held a certain pride.

She leaned back against the countertop, one slender leg crossed over the other and propped up on a finely pointed toe, and smiled uncertainly. "Actually, it's taken a very long time," she said. "Nearly three years in fact. But I'm finally getting there." She lifted her glass in a salute to herself, then drank deeply of its amber contents.

Evans sipped his and set it down again. "You seem very happy these days," he told her, remarking silently how odd it was that as she had grown happier, he had grown less and less satisfied with his own life.

She nodded and came away from the counter to sit in the chair opposite him. "I am," she admitted, "and do you know why I'm happy? Because I decided to be. Does that sound strange to you or, I don't know, disloyal?"

He shook his head. "No, not at all. I understand exactly what you mean by *disloyal,* but surely you've realized that Mark would want you to be happy."

"I hope so," she said, "but I'm not absolutely certain, really." She narrowed her eyes as if looking into the past. "Mark was ill, and that illness was so awful. He was in pain, and he was miserably disappointed, and he was frightened— and angry, angry at the illness, I suppose, angry at life, maybe even angry at God. At the time it felt as if he was angry with me, and I internalized that, swallowed it down with all the rest of the pain. I should have called him on it. I should have made him talk about it. Our last days together might have been happier if I had—and I would know now if his anger had really been aimed at me and why. I wouldn't have to wonder if he wished me ill or not."

"I can't believe he wished you ill!" Evans insisted, capturing her hand as it lay against the tablecloth. "He must have loved you. He *chose* you for his wife. You told me yourself that he went looking for a wife, and he settled on you."

She nodded. "Yes, I think he loved me, as much as he was able. I just don't know anymore how able to love he was." She smiled sadly. "All those years, and I don't know."

Evans didn't know what to say to that, not about Mark

Slater, anyway. He hadn't known Mark and wasn't in any position to judge the man now, but he knew something about Amy, something important. "Listen to me," he said softly. "I know you well enough now to know that you were a good wife to him. Whatever you think you should have done, you were the best wife to him that you could possibly have been at the time. I'm absolutely convinced of that. If you see things now that you might have done differently then, you must know that hindsight is simply a different perspective. Whatever you did, I know you did the very best that you could do at the time. You deserve to be happy, Amy. You must believe that."

She turned her hand over and clasped his. "Yes, I do believe that *now,* but thank you for saying it. I needed to hear someone else say it, someone besides Ruthie."

"Ruthie?" He seized on the name with absurd relief. "Oh, she's that friend of yours, the one who lives where? Marlow?"

"Waurika."

"Right. I still get mixed up." He curled a finger into her palm, trying to sound vastly more nonchalant than he felt. "Was she, um, your company night before last?"

She sat up a little straighter. Her gaze no longer held his. "No, that was another friend," she replied off-handedly.

"Ah." A man. He knew it with dead certainty, and he knew, too, that if he didn't get out of there at once he was going to make a fool of himself. He practically bolted. "Well, I'd better get going. You know how it is on your day off, a million things to do."

She got up and followed him into the hallway. "Is there anything I can help you with? I, um, like to stay busy."

He shook his head, not at all certain what urgent things he

was going to find to do. "Oh, that's all right. Enjoy your day. I'll see you, um, tomorrow night, I guess. I won't have time to run in the morning."

"Tomorrow night then," she said, sounding to him markedly unenthusiastic.

Irritation flashed over him. "Listen, if you don't want to run with me at night anymore, that's all right. I understand. You prefer the mornings, and I can't run most mornings, not in the cool of the morning, anyway, so if that's a problem, just say so."

She looked rather bewildered. "Oh, no, I love the night runs. I *make* myself run in the mornings for the extra toning, for the weight loss, actually," she muttered.

He didn't know with whom he was more exasperated, her or himself. He pushed away all the fears and irritations and forced a chuckle. "You don't need to lose any more weight. You look great as you are. And I'll see you tomorrow night."

She beamed at him. "Thanks. Tomorrow night, then."

He almost kissed her. He almost leaned forward and kissed her goodbye. With that near lunacy to spur him, he marched straight to the door and out of it.

Tomorrow night. He almost wished she *had* cried off—and didn't know what he'd have done if she had.

Chapter Eight

Amy took a deep breath, put on a bright smile and knocked firmly on the door. Evans opened it a heartbeat later. "Oh, hi!"

"Hi."

"What's up?"

She linked her hands behind her and widened her smile until her face hurt. "Not much. Just thought I'd come over and issue an invitation."

"Oh? Well, come on in. Someone I think you know is here."

Amy felt her smile falter as she cast a quick look over her shoulder. Sure enough, a bright red convertible was sitting at the edge of the curb across the street. Great, she could invite Evans Kincaid out to dinner with an audience. Terrific. She'd finally gotten fed up with waiting for *him* to say something, had even screwed up her courage to do the asking out herself, and he had company. Why in heaven's name hadn't she bothered to even glance at the street on her way over? *Because you were too busy keeping your knees from knocking together,* she told herself resentfully. Evans, meanwhile, had turned back into the house. She followed him timidly, wondering if it was too late to cut and run. Evans was standing half in the entryway, half in the living room, an arm extended in her direction even as he spoke to whoever waited inside.

"I assume you know my next-door neighbor, Amy Slater. Amy is, of course, Joan Shaw's sister."

Amy stepped into the curve of that proffered arm and found herself ushered forward. A tall, dark, extremely handsome gentleman was coming smoothly to his feet. "Ah, yes. How are you, Amy?" The Reverend Bolton Charles extended his hand. "You're certainly looking fine."

Amy felt a gush of unexpected pleasure at his compliment. "Why, thank you, Reverend Charles. You're looking nicely tanned yourself."

He shook her hand with a firm grip, then released it, and after a second, slipped his hand into his pants pocket. An awkward, confusing moment passed before she realized that both he and Evans were waiting for her to sit down! She promptly dropped unceremoniously into the chair, its telltale warmth telling her immediately that Evans himself had been sitting there. She popped up again, only to catch the men halfway down. Embarrassed, she dropped once more. The men were now standing again. Heat spread over her cheeks, and she pulled her feet beneath her once more, only to feel the weight of Evans's glare.

She smiled up at him weakly. "I believe this is your chair?"

"Not at all," he said firmly. "Please *don't* get up again."

She nodded self-consciously. The men sat down. What

followed was the most awkward quarter hour of Amy's existence. Her mind was so full of her misguided mission that she couldn't think of a thing to say to the well-meaning conversational forays of her two companions, until the reverend mentioned that he had hired Mattie to baby-sit his two children on occasion.

"Oh, Mattie loves children," Amy announced with some relief. "She'll make a wonderful mother."

"Not for several years, I hope," Evans said pointedly.

Reverend Charles ventured blithely onto contested territory. "Oh, you never can tell, really. None of us knows what the future will hold, not for ourselves and certainly not for our children. Now you take my father, for instance. He wanted me to be a professional baseball player, and just because I had the talent for it, he thought I was destined for it. I tried to tell him early during my college career that I felt a much stronger call to the ministry than sports, but he was so sure that my place was in a…more financially rewarding arena that he couldn't seem to hear me. I disappointed him dreadfully, and several years passed before he forgave me fully, years we can never get back, I'm sad to say." He slowed down to smile and concluded with "But we're fine now, thankfully."

Amy could tell that Evans was holding on to his temper by a thread. To his credit, however, he chose to chuckle mirthlessly and shake a finger at Bolton Charles. "My daughter," he said tightly, "has been speaking to you about speaking to me about this idiotic notion of hers of not wanting to go to college!"

Bolton sat forward earnestly. "I'm her pastor, as well, Evans, and all I really want is to mediate this dispute between you." He cast an apologetic look at Amy. "I wouldn't have brought it up in front of you, ma'am, but I know that she's been talking to you about it, and that you've given her good advice."

"And what advice would that be?" Evans demanded.

Amy looked him square in the eye. "I told her to at least try it, for the sake of peace if nothing else."

Evans deflated, groveling apologetically as he shook his head and rubbed his temples. "I didn't think you agreed with me on this," he said.

Amy sighed. "I don't actually, but I know how strong your feelings are on the subject."

His glare renewed, but after a moment he turned it on the minister. "And you, Bolton, where do you stand on this?"

"I think I understand both sides," he said calmly, "and because I can sympathize with both of you, I suggest a compromise."

"A compromise? How can you compromise on something like this? She either goes to college or she doesn't!" Evans exclaimed.

"Or," Bolton ventured casually, "she could wait a year and *then* go."

"Wait a year?" Evans exploded, jumping to his feet. "And do what? Paint her hair green and line her eyes?"

Amy felt her tongue moving before she could stop it. "That's not fair! She's modified her appearance considerably in order to mollify you."

"And I suppose I have you to thank for that!" Evans snapped, pacing back and forth in front of the coffee table.

Amy took umbrage. "Yes, you do, thank you very much! And I think Mattie's to be commended for trying to at least meet you halfway!"

"Halfway doesn't get her to college!" Evans roared.

"No, but it got her a job!" Amy shouted back before clapping a hand over her mouth.

Evans gaped first at her then at Bolton Charles. "Is *that* what it's all about?" he demanded of Amy. "You talked her into dressing like a sensible human being in order to soften me up about the job, is that it?"

For answer, Amy bit her lip and looked at her knees. Evans promptly turned on Bolton.

"Were you in on this?"

"I don't even know for sure what there was to be in on," Bolton said good-naturedly, "but I do know this, Evans. Mattie is a great deal more mature in some ways than her peers. I'll admit that the wild hair and extreme makeup threw me off for a while, but I've come to realize that it was Mattie's way of trying to make us see that she's *different.* I've said as much to her, and she commented wryly how ironic it is that no one seemed to recognize that difference until she started to look like everyone else. She said, too, Evans, that everyone seems to see her more clearly than you."

Evans rubbed both hands over his face and head. "What she doesn't understand," he said raggedly, "is that when I look at her I don't see just the girl she's become but the pretty baby she used to be, the toddler I read bedtime stories to, the little tomboy who used to scrape her knees, that fragile near stranger who cried her grief out in my arms when her mother died. I see *more* than everybody else, and more than anybody else, I want what's best for her. Why can't everyone understand that?"

"I understand it, Evans," Bolton said flatly. "Don't forget, I'm a father, too. But I'm willing to admit that parents don't always have the most dispassionate view of what's best for their own children."

"What possible harm can college do her?" Evans asked desperately.

Bolton shook his head. "I agree, going to college isn't a fate worse than death, but look at it from Mattie's point of view. Going to college keeps her in the slot of student, which she feels that you do not equate with the status of an adult. All she really wants, Evans, is for you to admit that she's growing up, that she has a right to make some of her own decisions. Give her a year to work after high school. She'll be much more amenable to college then."

"She'll be much more independent then," Evans countered. "She might even tell me to go soak my head when it comes time to keep her end of the bargain."

"Mattie has more integrity than that!" Amy said. "If she gives her word, then she'll keep it."

"How do you know that?" Evans insisted. "How can any of us *know* that?"

Bolton spread his hands. "Life doesn't come with any guarantees, Evans. No one knows that better than the three of us, having lost our loved ones to disease or accident, but I firmly believe that your chances of losing your daughter to acrimony is stronger if you pursue this course of no compromise than if you trust her to uphold her word. And think of this, Evans. You can't *make* her go to college now or later, but you can drive her away if you resort to ultimatums. If you can't agree to the year's respite, then please just let the argument wait until the end of this school year."

Evans stood dejectedly in the middle of the floor, his head bowed, forehead furrowed in worry. Finally he nodded, sighing. "Until March," he said. "I won't bring it up again until March. That will still give her time to apply and be accepted."

"If she chooses to do so," Bolton said mildly. He smiled in obvious satisfaction and deftly shifted the conversation onto a different track—a track that ran right over Amy. "Now, didn't I hear something about you coming to issue an invitation?"

"Oh." Amy felt her tongue thicken as her heartbeat sped up. "Uh, it's not…important. That is, i-it can wait until…"

Bolton slapped his knees with both hands and slid to the edge of his seat. "Until I'm gone," he supplied succinctly. "Forgive me, Amy, I'm not usually so obtuse."

"Oh, no, please don't go on my account!" she cried.

"I really should," he insisted.

"Stay, stay," Evans urged. "I put coffee on, if you'll remember."

"Amy obviously has something personal to ask," Bolton pointed out.

"No, I don't!" Amy denied instantly. "Uh, I just wanted t-to invite Evans…" She gulped. "A-and Mattie…I wanted to invite Evans and Mattie to dinner. Uh, I'd invite you, too, Reverend, but my little house won't—"

Bolton Charles held up a hand, chuckling. "That's quite all right, Amy, but please, call me Bolton. I've heard so much about you from the Shaws and the Kincaids that I feel I know you very well."

"Oh?" Amy looked at Evans, whose red ears seemed to indicate that he was embarrassed. Had he been talking about her to the rev—er, Bolton? Just what, she wondered, had he said?

"Yes, indeed," Bolton was saying. "You have some very ardent supporters, Evans and Mattie, Joan and Griff, even Danna. I can't tell you how happy she is that you've given up smoking, and it certainly seems to have agreed with you."

"Thank you," Amy murmured. "Thank you very much."

Bolton looked to his host. "Suppose that coffee's ready now, Evans? Why don't you check on it while I badger Amy about coming to church? I want to thank you for recommending us to the Kincaids," he said to Amy. "Now tell me how I can induce you to take your own advice."

Amy watched Evans leave the room before turning to the charming minister with a smile. "Actually, I think I may be ready to start attending church again," she said smoothly.

The reverend smiled as if he understood very well her reasons for coming to that decision, understood—and approved, though nothing in the next few minutes of conversation even obliquely alluded to a relationship between her and Evans.

Evans was still scowling when he returned with three cups of coffee on a tray. He slid the tray onto the coffee table and stood with his hands planted on his hips. "Anybody want cream or sugar?" It sounded so little like a polite query and so much like a dare that both Amy and Bolton burst out laughing. Evans didn't so much as crack a smile. He dropped onto the sofa, grumbling, "I'll be hanged if they aren't teaming up against me."

"Merciful heavens," Bolton Charles teased, helping himself to a steaming cup, "what is the world coming to? Your own pastor agreeing with your…" He flipped a look between Evans and Amy and smiled. "Your next-door neighbor." He made that last word sound far more intimate than it should, so much so that Amy felt herself blushing.

Was she that transparent? she wondered. And if Bolton Charles, who barely knew her, could see that she was falling in love with Evans, then Evans himself, who knew her so much better, could have no doubt of it. Suddenly, she wanted out of there. She sprang to her feet. "I, uh, have to be going. I…have things to do."

Bolton nodded sagely. "You'll want to start that special dinner for your guests."

Dinner! Tonight? Alarmed, Amy flew a glance at Evans, who sat up straighter and said exactly what she had thought. "Tonight?"

Amy gulped. "Well, i-if that's not c-convenient…"

To her dismay, he shrugged. "Fine with me…unless Mattie's needed to baby-sit?" That last he addressed to Bolton, who puffed his lips and shook his head.

"Not on my account."

Evans nodded as if that settled it. He looked at Amy. "What time?"

She couldn't seem to think. "S-Seven? Unless… Aren't you working?"

He shook his head. "Nope, I traded with a fellow. I was telling Bolton before you got here…" His voice trailed off, and suddenly Amy knew what he must suspect, that Bolton Charles had neatly manipulated both of them! "Seven will be fine," Evans muttered, frowning.

Amy wanted to cry. Wonderful! Now he felt trapped, no doubt. And what was the point anyway, with Mattie coming along? So much for her romantic dinner, for putting ideas in Evans Kincaid's head, for thinking she could pull off something so asinine! She mumbled a goodbye and hurried home, trying numbly to twist her mind around the evening's dinner menu, unaware that Evans's own feelings and assumptions closely matched her own—and went another step away from the mark.

* * *

Mattie was ecstatic, leaving little doubt in Evans's mind that Bolton Charles had duly reported the outcome of their little conversation, if conversation was the word for what had actually transpired that afternoon in his own house. He had been ambushed, caught in a neat crossfire of opposing forces. And just in case Bolton's salvo had not done the job of convincing him that he did not know what was best for his own daughter, there was Amy's impromptu little dinner party. The worst of it was, he had given his word. No wonder Amy had tried to wiggle out of the dinner date. Why even bother? But that made Bolton's obvious manipulation of this very event all the more puzzling. Obviously, he had had a double motive. Obviously, he was promoting a romance, and obviously his daughter was the co-conspirator in the latter case. And obviously, Amy was as uncomfortable about it as he was, even more so. Evans felt like wringing someone's neck; he just couldn't decide whose neck to get his hands around, his well-meaning but heavy-handed pastor's, his stubborn daughter's, or pretty Amy's. She *was* pretty, a fact about which Mattie seemed to want to gush.

"Honestly, Amy, I'm in awe. To quit smoking *and* to lose weight at the same time! You ought to write a book. Do you know how many people the world over would love to have your secret?"

"No secret," Amy replied succinctly. "I just got sick of myself."

"It's not just that you've slimmed down," Mattie continued, "it's the whole change. You're positively glowing! I mean, it's the same face, but there's something new about it. Your eyes are like jewels, I swear! And your skin's so pretty! Your teeth even look whiter!"

"Now we've reached the realm of the absurd," Amy said laughingly.

"No, really! It's like, I don't know, like the old Amy was just an imitation of the real thing."

"And moved on to science fiction!" Amy declared, then deftly turned the tables. "And look who's talking. You, my dear, have moved from radical rebel chick to wholesome, model-quality beauty. We're a pair of reformers, that's what we are, but I wouldn't want to have to compete with you in the looks department."

"Oh, but you could!" Mattie insisted. "Why, you look ten years younger now, at least!"

"Which would bring me nowhere near you, even if it were true!" Amy exclaimed, smiling.

Mattie made a face. "I hate being such a baby! Eighteen, ugh!"

Amy laughed and shook her head. "Mattie, you're the least babyish eighteen-year-old I've ever known."

Mattie leaned forward eagerly, one hand reaching across the small table for Amy's wrist. "Someone else must think so, too!" She hunched her shoulders, obviously holding some delicious secret close. At the last moment, she shot a nervous look at Evans, then came out with it. "Kate Novak's older brother Bailey wants to take me out!"

Evans sat bolt upright in his chair. "Novak. Is that the same Novaks from church?"

Mattie spared him a one-word answer, "Yes," and went right back to Amy. "I told you about Kate, remember? She's the girl who baby-sits with me. Well, we were walking home from the church nursery the other afternoon—they do an aerobics thing on Tuesdays after school and the moms pay us to watch their kids—and Kate says, 'I have to ask you some- thing. Can I give your phone number to my brother Bailey?' And I said, 'That's the one at OU, isn't it?' And Kate says, 'It's the funniest thing! He never liked any of my girlfriends before!' Anyway, he called me last night, and he's coming home on the weekend, and he wants to go out with me!"

"Oh, that sounds like fun," Amy said, "and you already know his family, and they know you."

"I've seen that guy," Evans put in, more and more irritated at the way he was being left out of the conversation, "and he's no kid. He must be what, twenty-one, twenty-two?"

Mattie shot him that old, rebellious look. "I didn't ask him that? What does it matter?"

"What does it matter?" Evans echoed, amazed. "He's too old for you, that's what it matters!"

Mattie rolled her eyes and went back to Amy. "He's majoring in social work, and this is his last year for that degree, but he wants to go on and get his doctorate in psychol- ogy."

"His doctorate," Amy repeated meaningfully at Evans. "Isn't that impressive?"

"It would be impressive," he growled, "if she was twenty."

"I'm going out with him, Dad, and that's final," Mattie said flatly.

Evans could only gape. "Who's the parent here, for pity's sake?"

"I knew you were going to be unreasonable about this," she retorted, flopping back in her chair and folding her arms. "Well, we just won't discuss it anymore."

He thought his head was going to explode. "We won't— God help me! Has the whole damned world gone cockeyed?"

"You don't have to cuss," Mattie said witheringly. Then she got to her feet, leaned over and kissed Amy on the cheek, and said oh-so-reasonably, "Thanks. Dinner was great. I'll talk to you later."

Amy patted Mattie's cheek. "You don't have to hurry off."

Mattie shot a glare at Evans. "Homework."

"Ah. Later, then."

"Thanks, Amy," Mattie whispered. "I can always count on you."

Evans bit his tongue until she got out of the room. "And she can't count on me? Is that what she's implying?" he demanded. "I'm just her father! Maybe I should move next door! Maybe I'd get some respect then!"

"You're being silly," Amy said quietly, which incensed him all the more, for some reason.

"Silly? I'll tell you what's silly, letting that girl go off with some college man is... No, it's not silly, it's dangerous, is what it is. It's irresponsible. It's—"

"Frightening," Amy slipped in bluntly. "It scares you to death, doesn't it, Evans, to realize that she's growing up, and there's nothing you can do about it, not a blessed thing."

He glared at her, knowing all the while that she was right and somehow unable to admit it. "You wouldn't understand," he muttered.

Amy looked away, but not before he saw the hurt in her eyes. "Because I don't have children of my own," she said. He started a clumsy apology, but she cut him off, her chin rising a notch, her gaze sharp as a needle. "You may be right. On the other hand, you were never a teenage girl."

He smiled lamely. She had him well and truly there. "You're right. It was a low blow. I shouldn't have said it. I don't know what happens to me when…when Mattie's concerned."

"I'm not telling you to completely let go, Evans," she said gently, "just loosen the grip a little, for both your sakes."

He closed his eyes and nodded. "I—I'll try."

"Great. Um, want some dessert? I have some of that fat-free dairy concoction that passes for ice cream."

He shook his head. "Naw, I'm not much in the mood for dessert. Dinner was good, though. It was real good."

"Thanks." She pushed her fork around her plate with the tip of her finger for a moment, then abruptly got up and carried the plate to the sink. She turned around, mouth open, a look on her face that told him she had something to say, but then she seemed to think better of it, clamped her jaw and slumped back against the edge of the countertop.

Evans searched his mind for something to say, pushing aside his concerns for his daughter. "Ah, are we on for our run tonight? I thought maybe we'd take it early."

She folded her arms across her middle, shaking her bowed head. "Not tonight. I think I'll just watch a little TV, listen to some music, maybe."

Did he hear the wistful tone of an invitation in her voice? He shook his head, remembering that she'd been maneuvered into this dinner. "Well, I'll just help you with the dishes and go then." He got up, his plate in his hand, but she shook her head adamantly.

"Oh, no. No. I won't hear of it."

He put the plate down again, unwilling to argue with her, uncertain what to do next. He didn't want to go, but she evidently didn't want him to stay. He stepped back. "I guess…I'll be seeing you."

She nodded. He stepped backward. "I'll, um, see you out," she said softly, brushing past him into the hallway.

She was standing at the door, holding it open for him when he got there, as if she couldn't get rid of him fast enough. He put his head down and walked through it, feeling lost and confused. She stepped out onto the porch and pulled the door closed behind her. He looked up in surprise as she stepped up next to him, wondering what she expected, what she'd been trying to tell him. Maybe he didn't want to know. He swallowed hard and forced a lightness into his voice that he was far from feeling.

"Well, thanks again for a fine dinner."

"My pleasure," she replied, sounding anything but pleased.

Not knowing what else to do, he started to turn away, but she stopped him, a hand on his shoulder. "Evans?"

He turned to face her, careful not to dislodge her hand. "Yes?"

She looked up into his eyes expectantly. "Evans, I never meant...that is, about tonight a-and Mattie..."

"I know." He sighed. "You only want to help. I'm going to think about everything you and Bolton have said, I promise. I'm going to do more than that, I'm going to pray about it very seriously."

She bit her lip and dropped her gaze.

Suddenly, he needed to make her understand things he barely understood himself, and he didn't know how to do it. He laid his hands on her, gripping her upper arms as if to shake her, and she looked up into his face again.

"Mattie's all I have, Amy," he said in a near whisper. "She's all I've had for so long. I want more, but I'm not sure I can have it." *You*, he thought. *What I want is you.* But the words were stuck in his throat, words that he had no reason to expect her to welcome. He could show her. All he had to do was bow his head and…but he couldn't help remembering what had happened the last time he had kissed her. She'd made it very plain that she wanted no part of him in that way. And he'd very nearly pressed himself on her again.

He jerked back so far that he had to hop down onto the top step to keep from falling off the edge of the porch. He tried to make it appear as nonchalant as possible, like he was simply ready to jog off home, but he knew, deep down, that it was useless. No matter how hard he tried, he wasn't any good at this buddy business. He wanted to love his neighbor, all right, but what he had in mind was not at all in keeping with the spirit of the Commandment—and not at all what his neighbor seemed to have in mind, either. They'd both be better off if he kept his distance from now on.

All these thoughts were tumbling around in his head as he flipped a jaunty wave at her and trotted off toward his own house. He didn't go home, though. He ran right on by his house and into the open field at the end of the street. He ran and he ran, without warming up, without his best shoes, without any destination at all, and when he couldn't run anymore, he sat down on a curb and put his head in his hands. Sometime later, shivering in the cold night air, he waved down a passing police cruiser and caught a ride home, taking some good-natured ribbing as his due. He didn't even look toward Amy's before he slipped into his own house.

The lights were off everywhere except Mattie's room and the kitchen. He went straight to Mattie's room, knocked on the door and opened it. She was lying on her belly on the bed in shorty pajamas that looked much like a soft knit short set. She looked up from the magazine that she was flipping through, shoved back her long hair and regarded him solemnly. She didn't ask where he'd been or what he'd been doing.

Evans fought down the impulse to clear his throat and simply said, "All the old rules still apply, young lady. I expect him to come inside, look me in the eye and shake my hand."

She didn't have to ask whom he meant. She said, "Of course."

"I want to know where you're going, how long it will take you to get there, and when you'll be home."

She shrugged. "So what else is new?"

"Another thing," he said, "I want you to stop treating me like the enemy just because I love you and want what's best for you!"

She sat up, put aside the magazine, and leaned forward over her folded legs. "Oh, Daddy," she said softly, "I don't like it any more than you do. Don't you know that if I could've kept from growing up, I would have, just for you?"

He felt as if she'd reached inside his chest and wrung his heart with her hands, and before he could recover from it, tears were rolling down his face. His first instinct was to back out and close the door, but she caught it before he could pull it shut and leaned against the door casing, her arms folded beneath what, he suddenly realized, were very ample breasts indeed. He stood in the darkened hallway and wiped surreptitiously at his face.

"You know," she said evenly, her voice pitched low, "it isn't like it's my first date. I know the rules, and I know how to take care of myself."

"I understand that," he said, wincing inwardly at the gruff sound of his voice, "but this is your first date since..."

"The rock freak," she supplied helpfully, a note of humor

in her tone, "yeah, I know. What you've never understood is that he was as basically harmless as I am." Her mouth actually crooked up into a smile. "He's probably wearing a crew cut and going in for tattoo removal by now."

Evans had to chuckle. "You think? After spending all that time looking like Attila the Hun?"

"It was a put-on, Dad!" she told him, giggling. "His parents hired an image consultant for him. At bottom it's that yuppie thing. Image is everything. Look like a rock star, *be* a rock star."

"No kidding?" He shook his head, laughing softly. "You mean his parents forked over good money so he could look like a freak?"

She laughed out loud. "Yeah, but that's not the point."

He sobered instantly. "What is the point, honey?"

"The point is," she said calmly, "you can't yank me up and move me halfway across the country every time I find a guy I like. For one thing, I don't have to go with you anymore, and for another, you can't live my life for me."

He sighed and lifted a hand to press against a temple pounding more pronouncedly every minute. "Is that what it's all about, Matilda? Do you hate me for bringing you here?"

"No! I like it here." She stepped forward and lifted a hand to his cheek. "And I love you."

He knew in that moment that it was going to be all right. He put his arms around her and hugged her close. "Aw, honey, I'm sorry. I guess I'm just not very good at letting go."

She laughed. "I've noticed that. But it's okay. You'll get the hang of it."

He set her away, his hands on her shoulders. When had it happened? he wondered. How had she grown up without him even noticing? It was true, though. She was a young woman, a beautiful young woman who'd make some lucky man a wonderful— He shut off the thought quite deliberately, but he knew it would be there waiting for him in the not-too-distant future. *One step at a time,* he told himself, *some big ones, some small.*

He chucked her under the chin, smiling. "You may have grown up practically overnight," he told her, "but you haven't grown up so much that the rules don't still apply."

She rolled her eyes and made a sigh into a major production, but a genuine hint of teasing humor came through in her drawled "Yes, Da-a-ad."

They were, perhaps, the two sweetest words he'd ever heard. Grinning, he kissed her loudly in the middle of the forehead and smacked her on the behind. "Go to bed."

"Yes, sir."

"And go to sleep," he amended as he sauntered past her in the hall.

"I will if you will," she called to him as he walked into his own room. "And, Daddy?"

"Yes?" He stepped out of one shoe and began easing off the other.

"Thank you."

He stopped right where he was and lifted his head. "For what?"

"Everything," she said, "but mostly for loving me no matter what."

Her door clicked shut before he could absorb that, let alone reply to it. He put his head back and let loose a long, cleansing sigh of relief, and then he closed his eyes and whispered, "Thank you, God."

Chapter Nine

He stayed away. He figured that God had been more than simply generous already. He and Mattie were closer than they'd been in a very long time. His little girl was gone, he realized that now, but the young woman whom she had become was a surprisingly engaging and interesting person. Everything would work out as it should now, he had little doubt of it, and Bolton had been right, of course. If he gave her the room she had requested on the subject of college, she would come around. How could he ask for more than that? Besides, it obviously was not ordained that he and Amy be together. She had just begun to live again; she needed— deserved—her freedom. And she had apparently been seeing some other guy. Why shouldn't she? They had no claim on each other. So he stayed away.

He didn't go out to run at night, choosing instead to wrench his exhausted body out of bed just hours after putting it there in order to pound the pavement before Amy's early-morning workout. He mowed her yard less often and never when she was around. With autumn on them, it was becoming less and less necessary, anyway. At least that's what he told Mattie when she asked. He told himself that when Amy called to ask why they weren't running together anymore he would pull not one but several excuses from the mixed bag he had prepared: he wasn't feeling up to it just now; he was tired; his work days were longer—never mind that he'd asked for the extra hours; the nights had grown too cool.

It was all true, and Amy must have realized that she didn't need to work out as often anymore, because the call he had expected, the call for which he had secretly hoped, never came. More proof, to Evans's mind, that Amy simply did not feel for him what he had come to feel for her. He had begun to pray to God that his feelings would change.

Ironically what changed merely made wrestling those feelings more difficult. For one thing, at the end of September, a superior on the Duncan Police Force retired earlier than expected, and Evans found himself working the coveted day shift much sooner than he'd planned. This made it possible for him to enjoy regular meals with his daughter— and spend his evenings in a torment of loneliness while Mattie baby-sat someone's kids or went out with friends, most of them older than her but thankfully not all male. She even went out twice with Amy, once to a movie and once to dinner. Both times she politely invited Evans to join them. Even Amy did so. But Evans knew that spending time with Amy would only add to the time it would take him to get over his disappointment, and he declined. He told himself that he ought to take a page from Amy's book and work at developing his own social life, but somehow he couldn't quite work up the necessary energy, despite the obvious incentive, made all the more intense when Amy started attending church.

She went alone at first, then showed up a couple of times with the Shaws, who literally beamed their pleasure. She seemed to relax after that and came along to service first with her friend Ruthie, a tall, painfully thin divorcée in her late thirties and then with a tall, blond, Greek warrior of a man named Stuart Bray.

Evans hated him on sight, even more than the pseudo rock freak whose attentions to Mattie had prompted Evans to yank his daughter up and move her halfway across the country. It didn't help that there was no reason for his deep dislike of Bray. The man was no threat to his daughter. His appearance was that of a conservative businessman, a very attractive conservative businessman, a very personable, successful and attractive conservative businessman. Joan knew him, so he was obviously an old friend. In fact, it was Joan who had the decency to actually introduce the man, and they had politely included Evans in their chat about other mutual acquaintances. But Evans couldn't stomach the conversation and walked away without excuse or apology. Later, when Mattie pointed out that he had been rude, Evans had said not one word, not in explanation, not in defense. What could he say when she was right, when explanation would damn him more than the offense itself? He didn't even know what to say to deflect her attention.

He began to think about going back to California. That wasn't the answer, and he wouldn't do it, not only because he couldn't be certain that Mattie would accompany him, and not because it would mean genuine financial distress, but because he liked Duncan. The neat streets and compact houses with their groomed yards shaded beneath sprawling trees by day and shadowed by lazy streetlights by night spoke to him of a peaceful, purposeful order that somehow meant home. The church with its welcoming, friendly members ever ready to lend a hand and its pastor, with whom a man could talk bluntly, offered a kind of security too seldomly found these days, even in one's own family. He didn't want to go, and he knew that he wouldn't, and yet he desperately needed to escape Amy's presence. Staying away was not the answer, but neither was leaving. Yet, he thought about California or somewhere else where Amy's memory could not go.

Amy's memory was not the problem, however. Amy was. No matter where he went, she seemed to turn up there in one way or another. Either she happened along, or someone mentioned her, or something brought her sharply to mind. Even on the Sundays he didn't go to church, which happened with increasing frequency as September began to slide into October, he couldn't escape her, for Mattie invariably sat with Amy on those days and chattered on afterward about what Amy wore and what Amy did and what Amy said. One thing Amy said, according to Mattie, was that she wished Evans weren't so busy, that she missed the "old times." To which Evans replied snappishly that they hadn't known each other long enough to have had "old times." But he missed them, too, those few weeks of buddying around, those easy times, young as they were. He missed them, but he couldn't get them back, for his feelings had gone beyond that easy camaraderie. He was in love with a woman who wanted him as a running buddy.

Not even a trip to the hardware store on his day off was safe. He found his sheet metal fasteners without bumping shoulders with her in the nuts and bolts aisle, but after wheeling through the drive-through for a soft drink and heading for home, he encountered her alongside the road, sitting on the trunk of her car and swinging her feet like a little girl with nothing more to do all day than dream. He wanted to stop. He wanted to drive on by—but he couldn't. The hood was raised. He whipped the truck over in front of it, stomping the brake with a vengeance, clenching his teeth against a curse. He couldn't have said which one of them he wanted to damn at the moment.

He bailed out of the truck and slammed the door, striding back to her. She smiled at him and lifted her hand in a little wave. She looked utterly delicious sitting there in slim, pale jeans, leather flats without socks, and a soft white sweater that barely covered her elbows and midriff. Her hair, more blond than light brown now, curled and waved softly about her delicate heart-shaped face. Her breathtaking eyes danced with him, smiling, warm. He ripped his shades off, in his most intimidating mood. "What the hell do you think you're doing?"

Unperturbed, she shrugged one shoulder, the wide, folded neck of her sweater sliding to expose one narrow bra strap. He gulped, anger and self-disgust dissolving in the potent brew of unrequited love and desire so physical it might have been a hand that reached out to clout him. He literally stepped back, as if he could remove himself from her orbit and gain control.

"Nice day, isn't it?" she said, looking up into the crystalline sunshine.

He frowned. He hadn't noticed. He didn't want to notice. He looked down at the car, as if gazing at the fender could tell him what was wrong with the motor. "Guess it's as good a day as any to have car trouble. What is it this time?"

She shrugged again. "I don't know. It just…stopped."

"Just stopped," he repeated, his voice conveying every ounce of his disdain at such a primitive, useless answer. "Cars don't just stop. They clank and stop. They grind and stop. They whine and stop. They sputter and stop. They even surge and stop. But they don't *just* stop."

"Well, this one did," she said cheerfully. "I was driving along, and the engine just shut off. I got it to the side of the road, which wasn't easy since the power steering locked, and tried to start it again, but it doesn't do anything."

He gave her a doubtful look and turned around to walk back toward the front of the car. "Does it click when you turn the key?"

She hopped off the trunk and followed him. "Nope."

"Hmm, how about a whir? Does it make a whirring sound when you turn the key?"

"Uh-uh."

"It doesn't make any sound at all?" he demanded, knowing he was being contrary but unable to stop himself.

"None," she said, "*nada,* zip, zero, no sound at all."

He lifted a skeptical eyebrow, opened the driver's door, got in and turned the key. It did nothing, made no sound beyond the workings of the mechanism as the ignition switch moved from one position to another. He fiddled with the radio knob and the light controls, trying to elicit some response…and failing. He got out of the car and walked around to the raised hood. He tapped battery cables and blew dust out of the distributor cap. He fiddled with the spark plug wires and inspected fuse boxes. In the end he could only glare at the offending engine and mutter, "Must be an electrical problem."

Amy sidled up beside him. "Can you fix it?"

"No."

She sighed. "Well, guess we'll have to have it towed."

We. He wanted to tell her to take *we* and stuff it, but he said, "Who do you want to call?"

She shrugged. "I don't know. Who do you think I should call?"

He sidestepped that. "Maybe you'd better let your brother-in-law handle it. I'll call him." He turned toward the truck, but she stopped him with a word.

"Can't."

He turned back, his athletic shoes scraping in the roadside gravel. "What do you mean, 'can't'?"

"Out of town," she informed him. "Idaho, I think Joan said."

Evans bowed his head. He didn't want to deal with this. He really didn't want to deal with this. He pulled his sunshades from his pocket and put them on. "Isn't there someone else I could call?"

She chewed her lip. "Well, I think Stuart's still in town, but I doubt he would know who to use around here for car repair."

"Stuart?" he scoffed, words exploding from his mouth as jealousy exploded in his chest. "That pretty boy couldn't fix a hairbrush, let alone a car! He wouldn't dirty his fingernails! He... He..."

She was laughing, had been laughing almost from the beginning. "Might mess up his manicure?" she supplied helpfully, giggling. "I know, it's awful, isn't it? I don't know how Becky stands it, except, well, they're two of a kind."

Evans had the strange feeling that he'd missed something somewhere. It was as if he'd been transferred supernaturally into a different conversation. "T-two...?" He swallowed convulsively. "Who...who's Becky?"

Amy smiled, brightly, brilliantly. "Why, Becky is Stuart's wife, of course."

"Wife," he repeated numbly.

"Umm. Well, they've been married for years. They were married just a few months before Mark and I. Mark always said that was what told him it was time to settle down, when Stuart tied the knot."

It seemed as if Evans was getting too much oxygen. His head was swimming, but it was not an unpleasant feeling. He tried to concentrate. "Stu— Mark and Stuart... They were friends?"

"Best friends," Amy confirmed, smiling still. "That's why Stuart feels obligated to look in on me whenever he's in town, you know."

Evans stared at her, confused now and not at all certain he wanted that confusion cleared up. "I'll...I'll call a tow truck," he muttered, turning blindly toward his own vehicle. He called a fellow whose name he remembered from the city's rotation list, was referred to someone else and finally found a driver who could come immediately. He got out of the truck and walked back toward Amy, who stood digging a toe in the dirt, arms folded, head bent. "Where do you want it taken?" he asked the top of her head, noticing the vibrant glossiness of the sun-streaked hair there.

She looked up abruptly, bright blue eyes smiling at him. "Oh, I don't know. The dealership, I imagine."

He nodded. "Good choice. This electrical stuff requires a real expert."

"I see. It's going to be expensive then, huh?"

"Yeah, I suppose so."

She sighed. "Well, maybe I ought to think about getting a

new one then. I mean, if I'm going to have to come up with a bundle, I might as well put it down on a new car, right?"

He lifted an eyebrow. "I don't know about that. Have you priced a new car lately?"

"Gone through the roof, have they?"

He snorted. "I gave less for my first house than I gave for that truck there."

Amy bit her lip. "That bad, huh?"

"I don't know what your financial situation is, but unless you have a *lot* of cash handy, I'd say you might be better advised to shop for a good used car."

She wrinkled her nose. "Isn't that kind of tricky, though? What if you get a lemon? I always wonder why somebody would get rid of a really good car, you know?"

"Lots of reasons," Evans argued. "Besides, if you know what you're looking for and you're patient, you can find a really good buy."

"But I don't know what I'm looking for," Amy countered, pinning him with that sharp blue gaze, "and I find that I'm getting less and less patient all the time." She said that last as if it related to *him* somehow, which made no sense at all.

He wrinkled his brow, trying to think through it, but it was so much easier to ponder the pros and cons of buying a used car versus buying a new one. He cleared his throat. "Well, just get someone who knows what he's doing to help you out."

"Okay," she said brightly. "How about you?"

If only he had known how like a frightened rabbit he suddenly appeared, eyes wide with that trapped-in-the-head-lights look, one nervous foot scrabbling for purchase. He even hopped back before he came to himself. "I...y-you...a relative is better for that sort of thing. Ask Shaw when he gets back."

She looked as if he'd slapped her. Bright patches of color suddenly burned high upon her cheeks, and a brilliant sheen coated her vibrant eyes. She opened her mouth, then snapped it shut again and turned on her heel. She was some distance away before he realized that she was going, just like that, leaving. For a moment, he could only gape, stunned beyond even thinking, but then it descended on him, the senselessness of such a reaction, unless…

"Amy! Amy, wait!"

She didn't so much as falter, her angry strides eating up a surprising amount of space. He went after her, running to catch up, aware that he was making a spectacle of himself on a busy street, worrying that he was making a mistake.

"Amy! Amy!"

She rounded on him as abruptly as she'd turned away. "I don't want to hear any of your excuses, Evans!" she snapped. "I've finally gotten the message, okay? We are *just* neighbors. That is all we will ever be." Her glittering eyes strayed away from him, and then she turned again and began to walk briskly, her arms swinging at her sides.

He was torn between following and turning back to see what had sent her off again. In the end, he did both, glancing back over his shoulder just as he stepped off after her, but then he stopped. The tow truck had arrived and the puzzled driver was climbing down from the cab, scratching his head at two abandoned vehicles. Evans growled in frustration. "Amy!" he shouted. "Your car!"

But Amy kept walking, her purposeful stride taking her farther and farther away. Evans started after her again, but then stopped and looked back. The tow truck driver was getting back into his cab. Blast! He threw a longing look in

Amy's direction, hearing her say again that they were just neighbors. He latched on to that last word. Neighbors. Yes, of course. Her house was just next door to his. He knew where to find her. Meanwhile, she was without transportation and somebody had to do something about that. Somebody had to take responsibility. He was good at responsibility, and he was a good neighbor. She'd remember that if he gave her a chance. He was sure of it. Almost with relief, he trotted back toward the vehicles, his hand raised over his head and waving.

"He's hurt, Amy. You won't talk to him, and he can't understand why."

He's hurt, Amy thought bitterly. *Well, what about me?*

She'd done everything she could think of to revive the man's interest, and she didn't understand why it was necessary to begin with. He'd kissed her before, before when she had been fat and drowning in self-pity and just plain not ready for it! *Now,* now that she was ready, now that she looked and felt better than ever before in her life, now that *she* was reaching out to *him,* he let her know in no uncertain terms that they were just neighbors and nothing more, never anything more. They weren't even running buddies anymore! She couldn't think what she had done that had so turned around his feelings.

Or had she read him all wrong from the beginning? Maybe that kiss had meant nothing to him, less than nothing, apparently. Maybe he liked the needy sort, the helpless kind of female that she had once been—except that she'd never really been that, no matter what he thought. She'd been morose and bitter and uncaring but never helpless. Whatever she'd been before, whatever she was now, it was by choice. It seemed to her that she had a *right* to feel bitter, to disappointment, to hurt. Those emotions even had a familiarity about them, a comfortableness. They brought with them the old urge to lock the door and shutter the windows and hibernate away from the world, nursing her wounds, keeping the pain alive. Aw, beans.

Sighing, she pinched the bridge of her nose and tried to formulate the right words and the right attitude to save them all further embarrassment and pain. After several moments, she dropped her hand and sent Mattie a wan smile. "I can't imagine what that man's thinking," she said shakily. "I haven't felt worth a darn lately, that's all."

Mattie's expression of reluctant confrontation became one of concern. She stepped forward and reached out a hand to feel Amy's forehead. Amy neatly sidestepped her, chuckling thinly. "It's not that kind of thing," she said. "It's…er, female."

"Ah." Mattie dropped her hand, nodding knowingly. Then she narrowed her eyes. "But that doesn't explain why you just walked away the other day."

"Oh, *that!*" Amy said, forcing a sound that might have been laughter. "I—I was just upset about the car, that's all. I needed some time alone to think about what to do, a-and I've found that exercise helps me think, so I—I just thought, why not walk home?"

Mattie seemed to find this reasonable. She pulled her feet up into Amy's armchair and settled in for a long, cozy chat. "So, what have you decided?"

"D-decided?" Amy echoed uncertainly.

"About the car. I don't care what Dad says, I'd go for a new car—that is, if you can afford it."

"Oh." Amy shook her head. "I haven't…um, that is, I've

decided to wait until Griff gets home and ask him for his opinion."

"I guess that makes sense," Mattie said, sounding a little disappointed. "Are you going to trade in your old car?"

Amy tempered her impatience. "I don't know. Why?"

Mattie shrugged. "Well, I thought, you know, if you weren't going to trade it in, maybe I could, like, buy it from you."

Amy couldn't help smiling. "Oh, like, buy it, huh?"

Mattie grimaced. "If we could talk Dad into it, that is."

"If," Amy reiterated.

Mattie sighed. "Last time we talked about it, he said that if I agreed to a year of college, he'd buy me a car. I haven't agreed…yet."

Amy's smile broadened. "But you are thinking about it."

"Yeah. I have to. He's been so reasonable lately, you know?"

"Glad to hear it," Amy told her, genuinely pleased and slightly amused at Mattie's predicament. Imagine having a reasonable parent!

Mattie bounced up out of the chair. "Well, I've gotta go." She wiggled her eyebrows, sparkling at Amy. "Got a date."

"Oh? Bailey Novak again?"

Mattie wrinkled her nose. "Bailey's a little too, well, intense, you know?"

"Meaning that you're not ready to be in love just yet?" Amy asked gently.

"Oh, I'm ready," Mattie said, her tone very matter-of-fact.

"Just not with Bailey," Amy surmised.

Mattie nodded. "Why is it that a perfectly nice guy who you like a lot just won't do?"

"I don't know," Amy said, shaking her head. "What makes

us fall in love with some people and not with others is one of the great mysteries, I guess."

"Well, it's awful when you can't fall for the right one," Mattie announced.

"It's worse when you can't help falling for the wrong one," Amy said softly.

Mattie cocked her head as if in thought, murmuring, "Yeah, I guess so."

Amy decided the conversation had gone far enough. She got up and escorted Mattie to the door. "Have fun on your date," she said, "and don't worry about falling in love. It'll happen when it happens."

Mattie pecked her on the cheek. "You know, I've missed my mom something awful," she confessed warmly, "but not nearly so much since I met you."

Amy caught her breath, tears building at the backs of her eyes. "What a sweet thing to say, but I'm just your friend, Mattie. Your mom should hold a special place in your heart."

"She does," Mattie insisted, "but so do you, a special place for a special friend." She kissed Amy once more, very gently, and then went out the door. She was on the bottom step before she called gaily over her shoulder, "I'll tell Dad he can come on over!"

The door was closed before the words fully registered. Amy yanked it open again and ran out onto the porch, crying, "Oh, Mattie, no! Not yet!"

Mattie was halfway across the yard, but she stopped and came back, peering at Amy through the deepening gloom of twilight. Amy felt like a worm under a magnifying glass and squirmed accordingly. "I—I'm just not...up to...a lot of company."

Mattie bowed her head, her hands going to her hips. "He misses you, Amy," she said softly, looking up. "He needs you."

Amy wrapped her arms around her middle. "No, he doesn't. He's made that perfectly clear."

"He's said the same thing about you, you know."

Amy laughed, not bothering to hide her bitterness. "What nonsense!"

"Is it?" Mattie asked incisively. "Seems to me that you were holding off the whole world with both hands when we first came here."

"Maybe I was," Amy admitted, "then. But not anymore."

"No?"

"No."

"Then Dad can come over whenever he wants, yes?"

Amy bit her lip. "Mattie, please try to understand. It's not the same thing as with you and me. It's…" She broke off, aware of the cunning look glowing in Mattie's eyes. Amy took a deep breath, knowing she was trapped, and forced as much lightness into her tone as she could manage. "Oh, why not? We…we're neighbors, after all. Neighbors ought to be able to come and go…pretty much as they please."

Mattie smiled. "I'll tell him."

"F-fine."

Mattie trilled a little wave and started off jauntily for home, leaving Amy to gulp down her panic as well as she could.

During the next few minutes, she thought about going out for a run or climbing into the tub or calling to ask her sister to come over, anything to derail a possible visit with Evans Kincaid. But trying to avoid Evans would just put the lie to everything she'd said to Mattie, and he would know then. He would know how desperate she was to fall out of love with him.

Chapter Ten

Evans didn't go over that evening. He was afraid to appear too eager, too *desperate*. And he didn't know what to say to her, how to approach her. His first impulse was to sit Amy down and tell her bluntly that she was hurting him, that he loved her, that he needed her. But what if she turned away? What if she walked away? What if she pushed away? How could he face such a possibility? It was easier to be turned away at the door, to have his phone calls cut off by feeble excuses and deadening clicks.

He'd had her car towed to the dealership. He'd instructed the dealer to call him with an estimate, had okayed the work and paid the bill, and then he'd arranged to have the car delivered to her as soon as the work was completed—and she'd greeted every word of that news with hems and haws and quick goodbyes. When she'd babbled something about paying him back the money he'd spent, he'd been the one to ring off abruptly. Just the suggestion that it was not his responsibility, his *right,* to pay for her car repairs hurt. He remembered the old VW Andie had driven when they'd met, all the hours he'd spent working on it, all the money he'd spent, money he didn't have to spare. Not once had she said anything but a heartfelt thank you, and every one of those had been accompanied by a warm hug and a kiss that would turn his thoughts to soft beds and wedding rings. With Amy he got Thank-you-very-much-I'll-send-you-a-check—click. Why on earth would any man in his right mind fall in love with that? Nevertheless, it wasn't Andie about whom he dreamed these nights, which only served to prove how perverse the heart was. Or something like that.

So he didn't go over immediately after Mattie explained, her tongue in her cheek, that Amy hadn't been feeling well but that she was now feeling more the thing. Instead of going over to her, he chose to pace the floor and tried to dream up scenarios that would have her falling into his arms the moment he did appear. Only after he'd exhausted those fanciful possibilities did he get down to the more serious—and seemingly impossible—task of trying to figure out what he was going to say to her when he did go over. In the end he decided to pick up where he'd left off several weeks before, and that was how he wound up standing on Amy's porch in his running gear at dawn.

He thought she would never answer the door, and when she finally did, her hair was all mussed and her eyes were only half-open. She was wearing lilac cotton pajamas tailored man-style, and one side of the collar was turned haphazardly. She looked utterly adorable, and it was all he could do to keep from pulling her into his arms and kissing her silly. Instead he chucked her under the chin, put his face close to her so he could be sure that she recognized him, and said, "How about it, neighbor? You up for a brisk morning run?"

She grumbled something about insanity, but the next moment she was looking at him with clear if ambiguous eyes. He heard himself saying, "I've missed you," and the next instant she was hurrying down the hall, calling over her shoulder that she wouldn't be a minute.

They ran to the park and back without stopping. Afterward they both were panting too hard to talk, gasping out goodbyes and see-you-laters as they parted company. Evans wanted to stay, catch his breath, and make her talk to him, but a glance at his wristwatch told him it would have to wait, and he supposed that was best, after all.

Ruth was at Amy's when he got in from work, but he stopped by for a quick hello, anyway, under the guise of asking if the shop had delivered her car okay, though it was sitting in the drive in plain sight. She insisted brightly that the old tin can was rattling like new, and when she ran for her checkbook, he ducked out, saying he had to start dinner, only to find Mattie at home with Kate Novak, the pair of them cooking up an experimental recipe. Evans sat down and ate the results, liked it well enough to lie about liking it better, and then learned that he'd get to eat it again on Sunday at the Youth Day Potluck Family Dinner at the church. Oh, yea. His enthusiasm for the notion perked up once he realized that it was the perfect excuse to pressure Amy to join them for dinner on Sunday. Mattie would undoubtedly be crushed if they didn't both praise her culinary efforts to the skies. If he worked it right, he might even get her to sit next to him in church, one small step for him that would undoubtedly go unnoticed by the rest of humankind.

He broached the subject of the Youth Day Potluck Family Dinner at the beginning of their run the next morning and received a shrug and a "sure" in response. Emboldened by such ease in attaining his first goal, he took the opportunity of pausing at the street corner to let a car go by to say, oh so nonchalantly, "You know, Amy, it's time you started babying that old car of yours. Maybe you ought to let her rest in and ride to church with us on Sundays." He didn't bother to tell her that more often than not, Mattie was with friends these days.

She rewarded him with a startled glance, which she followed with a smile. "Okay," she said.

He was so floored that she was halfway down the street before he caught up with her again. After that he decided not to press his luck, but on Sunday, when they were sitting shoulder-to-shoulder during the service, he went so far as to lift his arm and drape it casually along the back of the pew, curving it ever so slightly around her. Later, when they were sitting at the table in the fellowship hall with half a dozen other bemused adults trying to figure out exactly what they had on their plates, he patted her knee bracingly and left his hand there until she got up to go speak to her sister. He didn't have the nerve to try that again when she came back to her seat, but when they walked out to the truck later, he let his hand rest in the small of her back, and she made no objection. In fact, it seemed to him that she moved closer to his side, but when he squeezed her hand as he helped her up into the passenger seat of the truck, she studiously avoided his eyes, squelching his moment of hope.

He kept thinking about what she'd said that day the car had broken down for the second time. *"I've finally gotten the message. We are just neighbors. That's all we will ever be."*

Just neighbors. They hadn't been *just* neighbors from the moment he'd answered her first disturbance call. Didn't she know that? Not if she was as confused about his feelings as he was about hers. *All right,* he thought, *time to start clearing those muddied waters.* But what if what she saw was not to her liking? What if what *he* saw was not to *his* liking? Yet, how long could they go on in this manner?

By the time he slid beneath the steering wheel of the truck, he had decided to go slow, to take small steps toward his goal. If the pace was maddening, at least the risk was small. With that in mind, he closed the door, then reached across the seat to take her hand in his. She looked up in surprise, then dropped her gaze almost shyly. He gathered the words and dispensed them smoothly. "You know, Amy, it was never my intent to limit this relationship."

"No?" she said, her gaze lifting to meet his.

He brushed a lock of hair from her forehead, smiling. "No."

Her gaze skittered away, her teeth coming down on her bottom lip, as she softly breathed, "Oh."

He didn't quite know what to make of that, but at least she hadn't leapt out onto the tarmac and strode away. He started the truck and took them home in silence. When the truck rolled to a stop in front of the detached garage beside his house, he expected her to fairly leap from the cab, but instead she turned slightly in her seat, her gaze level and intense. "We are more than just neighbors, aren't we?" she asked softly.

He smiled and leaned close, his arm sliding along the back of her seat. "Yes, we are." He curled a finger beneath her chin and lifted it. "At least I hope we are." With that he brushed his lips across hers. When she did not immediately jerk away, he went back for more, but no sooner had his mouth settled over hers than her door swung open, her seat belt retracted, and she slipped out of his embrace to the ground. He viewed her through the opened door with a mixture of satisfaction and exasperation as he took in the glow of her face, the warmth of those magnificent eyes, the gentle curving of that luscious mouth, and the nervous, almost desperate, flutter of her hands as she waved goodbye and turned away.

Evans bowed his head, chuckling softly. One small step at a time, one small step after another.

The following days were among the happiest and most frightening of her life. They were more than friends. He had kissed her again. She was elated. She was terrified. She wanted time to stand still. She wanted to feel the exhilaration of standing on the precipice of love without experiencing the horror of plummeting over the edge. She wanted the thrill without the free-fall, the hope without the certainty. She wanted to see the desire in his eyes, feel him reaching out for her—and dance away before he could pull her in too close. It was perverse; she knew it was perverse, but in her giddiness she couldn't seem to find the strength to take the plunge.

She could feel his exasperation and his excitement. He called to invite her to dinner. She accepted happily, then schemed to include Mattie in the equation, or Griff and Joan, even Ruthie. Once she even sprang Stuart on him, but thankfully Stuart had the good sense to leave early, saying that he never quite found enough time to sleep on these sales trips and that "the little wife" would be expecting his call soon. Evans had gritted his teeth and managed to be civil. The next morning Stuart had called to chat before leaving town—and to tell her that the "overbearing cop next door" seemed to be controlling her life and exhibiting dangerous signs of jealousy. She had giggled and said, "I know," then had answered in the negative when Stuart asked if she and "the cop" had an understanding.

Stuart wasn't the only one who didn't understand what was going on. Amy didn't really understand herself. She loved Evans. She trusted him. She wanted him in her life. So why was she so afraid to take that next step? It wasn't a matter of veering between one emotion and another. Every moment of every day she both loved and feared loving Evans Kincaid. So he reached out with increasing exasperation, and she danced away, reveling in the brief contact and constantly eluding it. Yet, sometimes, despite her fears, she cut it too fine, like the morning of Evans's day off.

It was his habit on his day off to come over about a half hour later than on a work day for their morning run. That extra thirty minutes gave him the illusion of sleeping in without costing him his morning, he said, and on those days their runs were always lazier and more playful. It was just so on that particular morning. The weather was crisp, but Amy had warmed up enough to shed the fleece sweatpants she'd put on over her spandex biking shorts. She answered the door in battered shoes and white socks with the tops neatly folded down, black biking shorts and a roomy pink, long-sleeved sweatshirt worn over a little black latex top that took the place of a bra and did dual duty as an undershirt. She'd pulled her hair into a ponytail and held the shorter curls back from her face with a thick black headband. Evans lifted both brows in appreciation and bowed her out the door, smiling.

She didn't even give him time to finish his warm-up, just

trotted down the steps and took off. He caught up and passed her, then turned and jogged backward for a few paces, grinning and saying, "Good morning, good-looking."

She laughed and picked up the pace, leaving him behind easily. He turned on a little speed and caught up. She turned on more, and they ran so for some time, until they reached a small, open field just short of the park. There the exhilaration got the better of her. "You're losing it, Kincaid," she called over her shoulder. "I can't believe it! I've finally outpaced you!"

He was beside her in a flash. "You're dreaming, sweetheart." To prove it, he sprinted ahead, slowing only when he turned around, jogging backward.

"Oh, yeah?" she teased, catching up with him in a burst of speed. He was breathing hard enough to boost her confidence. "I suppose," she said panting, "you *let* me run ahead of you."

He flashed her a grin. "Darn right I did."

"Oh?" She backed off a little, pacing herself. "Why… would you…do that?"

"For the view, of course."

She stumbled, elation shooting through the core of her. He caught her and they fumbled to a stop. "Not," he said between gasps, "that the view from the front isn't as appealing. I just can't outpace you very long *backward*." She put her head back and laughed in delight. His grin froze, his gaze going to her mouth. Anticipation shivered up her spine, but when his head began to lower, she laughed again and shoved him, sprinting past as he went down.

"Hey!" He was up and after her almost instantly. Catching her with ridiculous ease, he scooped her off her feet and whirled her around. She screamed in delight, her arms clutching him about the neck, and then he stopped and dropped her against him, his arms holding her loosely as her body slid along his toward the ground. Her sweatshirt rucked up. Her heart pounded with more than mere exertion as she looked up into his face. "Amy," he whispered, and then his mouth was on hers, quickly growing fierce as his arms tightened about her.

A honking car had them leaping apart. Evans caught her hand, shooting an irritated look at the laughing occupants of the passing car while color bloomed in her cheeks. He was smiling when he looked down at her again, though. "I don't care," he said softly. "Do you?"

She didn't know how to answer him. It was such a loaded question, perhaps more so than he knew. She reverted to the steps of the dance she'd invented for them. Flashing him a mischievous smile, she shook free of his grasp and sprinted ahead toward the park. But he didn't immediately join in this time. Instead, he stopped where he was and brought his hands to his hips, head bowed, one knee cocked. A wave of alarm shivered Amy, but she just tugged at the bottom of her sweatshirt and kept running.

Eventually he caught up to her, but not before she'd reached the park and slowed to a walk. He smiled at her, but the smile was wan and introspective as he turned at once for home. Disappointment came. She had had visions of lingering in the park to tease and dance, but maybe it was best this way, after all. She couldn't help noticing that some of the sparkle had gone out of the morning, and in its place a new fear had come to hover near the back of her mind. How long, it whispered, before he tired of the game, before she danced alone?

* * *

Evans groaned as the aspirin slid down and he straightened up his head. He hadn't slept a wink the night before, and his body ached with the flush of fever. He could feel the congestion building behind his nose and below his eyes again. It would be hours yet before he could take another dose of the decongestant. The annual office cold, the guys on the force had called it. He called it misery, sheer misery. With a sigh, he dropped into the chair beside his bed and began unlacing the shoes he had just tied. No run for him this morning, no matter how much he wanted to see Amy. He glanced at the clock on the bedside table. Twenty-five minutes late already. She'd be worried, and if she knew that he was feeling ill, she'd be doubly so. What to do?

After sitting with his head in his hands for several minutes, he got up and padded in his stockinged feet to Mattie's door. He knocked, turned the knob and stuck his head inside. Mattie rolled over and pushed her hair out of her eyes, peering at him sleepily. "What's wrong, Dad?"

"I've got the crud," he said, wincing at the nasal sound of his voice. "I feel awful, and I need you to call Amy for me."

"Why not call her yourself?" she asked around a yawn, sitting up.

He grimaced. "I don't want her to know I'm ill. She'll just worry."

"You want me to lie to her?" Mattie asked in surprise.

He shook his head, groaning with the pain of the motion. "No, no," he gasped. "Just tell her I can't run this morning, say I got up late. That much is absolutely true. Just don't mention that I'm going back to bed with a splitting headache and a stuffed-up nose. Okay?"

"If you say so," Mattie replied doubtfully, "but what about tomorrow?"

"Just do it, baby," Evans said. "I'll sleep this thing off today and be up for the run tomorrow as usual."

"I think you're kidding yourself," Mattie said, throwing back the covers, "but it's your head."

"My splitting head," he murmured, shuffling back down the hall to collapse upon his bed. He lay there in a stupor of misery until Mattie came to tell him that Amy had sounded disappointed but understanding on the phone.

"I'm betting she'll be over as soon as you supposedly get home from work," she told him.

He said his thanks into his pillow, then forced himself some minutes later to sit up long enough to phone his boss. Mattie brought him a glass of warm milk and whiskey laced with honey and mint from the years-old bottle of her mother's favorite remedy. He drank the milk and left the whiskey on the night stand. He was asleep when Mattie came to whisper goodbye as she left for school.

He woke hours later, swallowed more aspirin and decongestant, and after moaning in bed for a while, realized he was feeling better and got up. He threw a hooded fleece jacket on over his running shorts and T-shirt and padded into the kitchen to make himself a cup of hot coffee and a mug of chicken noodle soup. Thus fortified, he adjourned to the living room to lounge and sip and flip through the channels on TV. He was considering a hot soak in the tub when Mattie came in.

She hung her sweater on a hook inside the coat closet door, deposited her school books on the top shelf and came into the living room to kiss his forehead. "Hi, Dad. Feeling better?"

"Yeah, some."

"You don't have a fever."

"Good. Now if I could just shake this blasted headache…"

"Give it time. Have you taken anything?"

"Umm-hmm, but it's time to take it again, I think."

"Tell me where it is, and I'll get it."

"On my bedside table."

"Be back in a flash." She was good as her word. Unfortunately, by the time she got there, he was sneezing his head off. "Try to swallow these while I get some tissue," she said, dumping the pills into his hand.

He threw his head back and popped the pills into his mouth, while she hurried into the other room in search of facial tissue. She was barely out of sight when the doorbell rang. He groaned and tried to decide which would hurt worse, calling Mattie back to answer the door or answering it himself. Before he could decide, however, the door opened and Amy walked in, calling, "Mattie?"

Evans groaned, knowing he was in for it now. Amy spun around in the entryway, peering into the living room. "Evans?"

He closed his eyes, sighing. "Hello, sweetheart."

"What's wrong with you? Why aren't you at work?" she demanded, coming into the room.

"Oh, rot," he muttered. "I didn't want you to know."

"Know?" she echoed, stepping closer.

"It's just a headache," he said, hoping to downplay what was turning into a tiger of a cold, and for emphasis, he closed his eyes and let his head drop back onto the chair.

He knew it was a mistake the instant he heard her gasp, and in an effort to allay her fears, he sat forward too quickly, pain slicing through his head. She did not miss his wince nor the significance of it.

"My God!" she gasped. "How long has this been going on?"

"Not long," he said, trying to sound unconcerned and sounding weak instead.

"Have you been to a doctor?" she demanded.

"No," he admitted. "There's no point—"

"You need a doctor!" she cried. "You can't ignore this kind of thing!"

"It's just a headache," he insisted, adding sheepishly, "maybe a cold."

"Just a headache?" she exclaimed. "That's what Mark kept saying! 'Just a headache! Just a cold! Just a bug! It'll go away! I'm fine!' But it didn't, and he wasn't! Oh, God, how can you do this to me?"

"No one's doing anything to you," he said placatingly. "I just picked up a virus that's going around work. Calm down, or you're going to be sicker than I am."

"Calm down?" she echoed bitterly. "I can't calm down! Don't you see? I can't do this again. I can't bear to even think…"

"Amy!" he scolded, shooting up to his feet. Wrong move. A hammer descended, nearly knocking him to his knees. He moaned and swayed, eyes gone glassy. "Amy!" he gasped, but when he reached for her, she jerked away. In a moment of clarity, he saw the unreasoning terror in her eyes, the heartbreaking fear of loss, the helpless love. Despite the physical misery, he felt a moment of such relief and joy that he nearly laughed, but then Amy turned and fled, slamming out of the house and, he had no doubt, out of his life. *If* he let her get away with it, that is, which he had no intention whatsoever of doing. He'd had enough.

"Enough what?" Mattie asked, a box of tissue in one hand, perplexity on her face.

"Enough…of everything!" he shouted at her, ignoring the

fresh pain in his head. "Enough wanting and not having! Enough loving in silence! Enough sleeping alone! Enough… of enough!" He snatched a handful of tissues from the box and swiped them at his nose before stuffing them, balled, into his pocket and stomping out of the house.

The brittle autumn grass pricked the soles of his feet as he stomped across it in his socks. He paid it no more mind than the scent of burning leaves in the crisp air or the waning throb in his head. He had come to the end, the utter edge, of his patience. He pounded up the steps and across Amy's porch, wrenched the door open and strode inside, totally unaware of the absurd picture he made, his unshaved jaw clenched stubbornly, his dark hair tousled and spiked, his hooded fleece jacket—its pocket bulging with tissues—doing nothing to hide the rumpled T-shirt and shorts beneath it, his stockinged feet bare of shoes and dirty, flecked with tiny, strawlike pieces of grass. A casual observer would have labeled him a madman, a madman with a case of the sniffles, perhaps, but a madman, nonetheless.

He walked purposefully through the house, looking for her first in the living room, then the kitchen, bath and finally the bedroom. She was sitting on the edge of her bed in jeans and a sweater, holding a framed photograph in both hands, tears running down her face. A drawer was open on the bureau next to the bed. Evans's anger drained away, but the determination stayed. He walked softly to her side and glanced down at the photo of her late husband, then he took it from her hands, placed it face-down in the drawer and slid the drawer shut. She covered her face with her hands and wept. Gently he drew her up to her feet and pulled her against him, his arms crossed in the small of her back.

"Look at me, Amy," he said. His tone, while soft, brooked no argument.

Sniffing, she dropped her hands to his shoulders and turned her face up. "I'm sorry," she began tearfully, "but I just can't—"

He tightened his hold on her, cutting off whatever inane words she'd been about to say. He didn't mean to hear them. He would not hear them. This time Amy was going to hear *him,* really hear him.

"I love you," he told her flatly. "I'm tired of loving you and wanting you and never quite having you, Amy."

"Oh, Evans." She started to weep, crumpling against him.

He used one hand to force her chin up and make her straighten enough to look up at him. "I'm not doing this anymore," he said. "I'm not indulging your fears or chasing any more ghosts. From this moment on, Amy Slater, you're mine. Get used to it."

He recognized the struggle taking place behind those bright blue eyes, brash-new desire battling old fears. It was a battle he meant to see go his way, and he lifted a brow intimidatingly, falling into the role of enforcer with the ease of long practice. To his surprise and everlasting relief, Amy's mouth quirked up into a smile.

"Are you going to handcuff me, Officer?"

He fought a smile of his own and gave her a stiff nod. "If I have to."

"Are you sure you're up to it?" she said, her teasing tone heavily laced with concern. "You're sick, after all."

"I have a cold," he said, dropping his gaze to her mouth warningly, "and I'm just about to give it to you."

"Oh?" She slid her arms around his waist.

"Umm-hmm. We'll be sick together," he promised, bringing his mouth within a breath of hers, "and then we'll be well together."

She stared up into his eyes for what seemed an eternity, but then she whispered, "As long as we're together," and lifted her chin.

He made that kiss a seal, knowing that the final battle had at last been fought and the war had been won. It was the first time in his life that he'd ever thanked God for a cold, but he would never sneeze again without thinking how a common virus had laid bare Amy's final fear so love could build the bridge that brought their two hearts together.

Amy rubbed her nose with a tissue that felt like a wad of sandpaper and groaned, "I feel awful. Do you feel this awful?"

"Nope. I feel fine."

"Liar."

He bent and kissed her firmly on the mouth, then shoved a mug of steaming brown liquid at her and said, "Quit complaining and drink your tea."

She snuggled into the corner of the sofa, smiling despite the third day of misery. In truth, he was all but well. He could have gone to work if he'd wanted to, but he'd preferred to stay home and play nursemaid one more day. She sighed and laid her head on his shoulder when he sat down next to her. He gave her knee a squeeze, reached for the notebook at his side, and propped his feet on her coffee table. "Now then where were we?"

Amy rolled her eyes and sipped her tea. "I have to think about this, Evans. These aren't simple decisions."

"Seems simple enough to me," he said. "I love you. You love me. Now what day do you want to get married?"

"I don't know," she said. "As soon as I'm well."

"That's no answer, Amy," he exclaimed, laying aside the notebook once more.

"Oh? And I suppose you can do better?"

"I certainly can."

She ignored that, saying, "If you'd just be reasonable and give me a month or so, I could plan a small, wonderful wedding for us."

He turned slightly on the couch, facing her. "Do you want to sleep alone for the next month?" Her mouth curled up on one end, and she shook her head, her eyes going all dreamy. He sat back and pulled her head down onto his shoulder once more. "Good. Neither do I. Now sip your tea and let me handle this."

"Yes, sir, Officer, sir," she quipped, not believing for a moment that he could do it.

He proved once again that she had underestimated him. Picking up the receiver of the telephone that sat on the table next to his feet, he punched in a number and waited. "Hello," he said after a moment, "I'd like to speak to the Reverend Charles, please. Evans Kincaid. Thank you." He dropped a kiss on the crown of Amy's head and quickly spoke into the telephone. "Bolton? How are you?" He chuckled. "Yeah, I hear it's going around. Well, listen, think you'll be over it by a week from today?"

"A week?" Amy squeaked. He hushed her with a finger laid across her lips.

"Oh, nothing much," he said in reply to something the minister had asked, "just thought you might like to perform a simple wedding… Yeah, mine." He laughed again. "Who else? Kind of adds new meaning to the idea of loving your neighbor, doesn't it?"

Amy cradled her cup against her drawn-up knees and slipped an arm about his shoulders. A week! She wondered if she'd be up to shopping tomorrow.

"Sure thing," Evans was saying. "Well, we'll want our families there, of course, Mattie and the Shaws and Amy's parents. I was thinking that Danna would make a pretty flower girl, and Mattie would love playing bridesmaid. Might as well let Joan and Griff do the honors."

He cocked an eyebrow at Amy, who smiled and nodded happily. A week wasn't too soon. A November wedding. Well. She'd call the bakery right away and her parents immediately afterward. Oh, boy, were they going to be surprised! She wasn't worried, though. She knew they'd love Evans and Mattie both.

Evans put his hand over the mouthpiece of the telephone receiver and said to her, "Bolton thinks he knows where you can buy some real nice ready-made silk flower arrangements, some bridal shop near downtown. Interested?"

"Absolutely."

He picked up the notebook and plucked a pencil from behind his ear, saying into the telephone, "Shoot." He scribbled down the name and address, then passed the book to Amy. She recognized the name of a prominent member of the church and knew immediately which shop was hers. She should have thought of it sooner.

"Music?" Evans said, looking to her. She shrugged. "Hmm, we'll have to get back to you on that one," he told Bolton. "Better give me the name of the organist, though.

Maybe she can suggest something." He grabbed the notebook back and scribbled another note, then said, "Oh, and I suppose the boys at work will want to make up some kind of honor guard." He talked a moment longer and hung up. "See, there, that wasn't hard at all."

"Honor guard!" Amy exclaimed. "Evans, what am I going to wear to a wedding formal enough to have an honor guard?"

He shrugged negligently. "I don't care. Wear your running shorts, if you want. I like the way you look in them. Of course, I'll be wearing full dress uniform, but don't let that bother you."

Her jaw dropped. "Evans! You don't expect much, do you? Just a full-blown wedding in a week!"

"It doesn't have to be all that much," he said, taking her hand in his, "but I want it to be all it can be. I know it won't be the grand ceremony you probably had with Mark, but I'm just not willing to wait for that."

She smiled and brushed his cheek with the back of her fingers. "No," she said, "it won't be the grand ceremony I had with Mark. It'll be the grand ceremony I'll have with you. I can't ask for more than that."

He kissed her, sliding his arms around her. When it was over, she leaned into him, her head on his chest. For a long while, he stroked her hair while she made mental lists of everything that would have to be done. Then suddenly he asked, "Do you think he would approve of this? Us, I mean."

She lifted her head. "Who?"

"Mark."

She thought a long time before answering him. "Yes, I think he would, because he did love me. Not the way you do,

I don't think, but in his own way and as much as he was able." She looked at Evans, her heart in her eyes. "And I loved him," she said simply, "not as much, perhaps, as I meant to, but enough that some part of me will go on loving him always, not so much, though, that I can't love you with my whole heart."

He nodded. "I understand perfectly. It was the same way with Andie and me. We loved each other as much as we possibly could then, knowing what we knew then, being who we were. Yet, somehow, Amy, I can love you more now because of her, because of what she and I had together. Do you know what I mean?"

Her eyes filled with tears, but she would not allow them to fall. Happy tears didn't have to fall. She smiled, completely forgetting how awful she felt and how little time she had before the wedding. "Yes," she said, "I know exactly what you mean, now."

He swept a lock of hair off her forehead, skimmed the line of her nose with his fingertip, tapped her lower lip gently. She knew just what he was thinking, and no, a week wasn't too soon. He smiled as if reading her thoughts, then settled down into place once more.

"Drink your tea," he said. Then, just as she lifted the cooling brew to her lips for a good slurp, "I laced it with whiskey and mint…" She spluttered and almost choked as he added, "Just in case I had to get you drunk to make you agree!" Her mouth dropped open. "Well, I didn't want to wait more than a week," he said defensively. "Besides, the stuff is good for you. I think. I've never been able to get much of it down myself to find out." His grin was just apologetic enough to be believable.

Amy put her head back and laughed. It was a sound she was going to be making a lot from then on. She knew it…in her heart. Where it counted most.

* * * * *

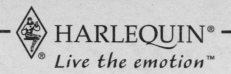

HEARTWARMING INSPIRATIONAL ROMANCE

Contemporary,
inspirational romances
with Christian characters
facing the challenges
of life and love
in today's world.

**NOW AVAILABLE IN REGULAR
AND LARGER-PRINT FORMATS.**

Steeple
Hill®

HARLEQUIN®

Super Romance®

...there's more to the story!

Superromance.
A *big* satisfying read about unforgettable
characters. Each month we offer *six* very different
stories that range from family drama to adventure
and mystery, from highly emotional stories to
romantic comedies—and much more! Stories
about people you'll believe in and care about.
Stories too compelling to put down....

Our authors are among today's *best* romance
writers. You'll find familiar names and talented
newcomers. Many of them are award winners—
and you'll see why!

If you want the biggest and best
in romance fiction, you'll get it
from Superromance!

Exciting, Emotional, Unexpected...

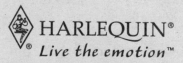

HARLEQUIN®
Live the emotion™

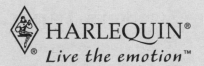

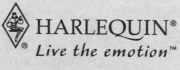

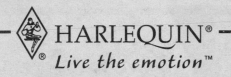

SPECIAL EDITION™

Emotional, compelling stories that capture the intensity of living, loving and creating a family in today's world.

Modern, passionate reads that are powerful and provocative.

nocturne

Dramatic and sensual tales of paranormal romance.

Romances that are sparked by danger and fueled by passion.